Madge

RING OF CRYSTAL

Much as Annie loved her mother, she did wish she wouldn't keep matchmaking on her behalf. Most of all she wished she wouldn't try to throw her at the forceful Adam Corbett. Because, for the first time in her life, Annie had fallen in love—and it was a situation she didn't know how to handle . . .

Books you will enjoy
by JANE DONNELLY

FACE THE TIGER

To get over the disappointment of realising that her beloved Peter had no intention of marrying her, Sophy got a job working for the devastating Gavin Tighe—who told her, 'Don't underrate yourself.' But that wasn't so easy to do, when everyone thought you were nothing—including Gavin!

A FIERCE ENCOUNTER

Perhaps Lacey Allen had expected too much of her brief and blazing affair with Martin Jackson; at any rate he had taken himself off and she had seen nothing more of him. Now, five years later, he had turned up again; and Lacey was older and wiser now and she was not going to let him upset her. But could she be *quite* sure about that?

MOON LADY

It didn't seem to matter that Jake Ballinger was a wealthy tycoon and Prudence Cormack a comparatively ordinary girl; from the moment they met there was an undeniable chemistry between them. But was a man like Jake really likely to be interested in her? Wasn't he merely charming her into selling him her cottage? And where did Tanya Merrick fit into it all?

RING OF CRYSTAL

BY

JANE DONNELLY

MILLS & BOON LIMITED
15–16 BROOK'S MEWS
LONDON W1A 1DR

First published in Great Britain 1985
by Mills & Boon Limited

This edition 1985

ISBN 0 263 74988 6

Set in Monophoto Times 10 on 11 pt.
01–0385 - 58937

Made and printed in Great Britain by
Richard Clay (The Chaucer Press) Ltd
Bungay, Suffolk

CHAPTER ONE

'ANNIE, you're going to be late.' Her mother's voice with its soft Welsh lilt reached her, the same words of affectionate chiding that she had heard almost every morning for more than ten years.

'Coming!' Anna Bennett called breathlessly, and speeded up her aerobic work-out: ten jumping twists, heels up, knees up, jogging on the spot. Ten minutes later she dashed down the stairs and into the kitchen where her parents sat at the breakfast table.

This was how every morning started. In this room with the warm stripped pine cupboards and chairs, and the dresser with the old willow pattern plates and dishes going back three generations. The tablecloth was blue and white check and there was a fragrant arrangement of honeysuckle and pink rosebuds in a crystal bowl.

Douglas Bennett was finishing his bacon and eggs, and scanning his newspaper at the same time. Catrin was drinking tea and reading out a letter to him, and when Annie whirled into the room they both smiled at her.

'You'll come through the ceiling one of these mornings,' her father warned her, and Annie grinned.

'Sorry, did I make the light swing?'

Exercise and health were making her skin glow. Her eyes were hazel, very bright and clear, and her dark hair shone. She was a small, slender, enchantingly pretty girl.

Her parents had married late. When Catrin became pregnant at forty both she and Douglas knew the risks, but a perfect little girl had been born, their own small miracle, and they were besotted with her. If her nature had not been basically sound she would have developed into a horror. In fact she always had plenty of friends, because she was kind and life around Annie was usually exciting. Sometimes too exciting. She did not always bring out the best in her admirers. Her current date was becoming unbearably possessive and the evening had ended in a jealous scene.

'What time did you get in last night?' her father enquired.

She was only just breaking them of the habit of sitting up for her. She always felt guilty when she came in late and found them nodding in front of the fire and a blank television screen. They were older than the parents of any of her friends, and dates were often spoiled for her because she knew she was keeping them up.

She had argued in her late teens when her mother had insisted that they liked to know she was safely at home before they locked up for the night, but for the last three years her work as a journalist on the local newspaper had meant some unsocial hours, and very gradually—so long as they thought they knew where she was and who she was with—they had given up waiting for her.

She kept them informed. She brought her friends home for inspection and she told them nothing that might disturb them. Her father had had a slight heart attack within a month of retiring from his job as advertising manager on the newspaper where Annie worked, and Annie would have gone to almost any lengths to avoid worrying him, so she hid her problems, large and small, from them. Now she gulped her coffee and leaned over her father's shoulder to read the headlines and told them, 'I wasn't late.'

'He's a nice young man,' said her mother.

Huw Sanders was honest and generous and eligible, and he and Annie had been dating ever since she dropped a glove in a revolving door, stooped to pick it up, and Huw gave the door a hefty shove that shot her full length into the foyer of the Grand Hotel.

He couldn't apologise enough, while he helped to collect the contents of her handbag.

'Are you all right?' he kept asking.

'That's a damn silly question,' said Annie, filled with the irrational rage of someone who has been made to look an idiot, even if it was by accident. Then she smiled, 'Yes, I'm all right. When you push a door you push, don't you?'

Willing hands were helping her up, all the available staff had rushed forward. Everyone in the foyer had seen her come hurtling in, head first. It was comic, as she was young and obviously unhurt, and she brushed herself down, and said, 'Sorry about that,' to the manager. 'Forget it,' she said to the man whose name she didn't know at that stage. 'No harm done,' then she went into the kitchens to interview an apprentice chef who had won second prize in a TV competition for pastrycooks.

Back at the office she found a bunch of flowers waiting on her desk. It had been handed in at Reception with a sealed note for Miss Anna Bennett.

The note apologised again, was signed Huw Sanders, and said he hoped he might phone her and that he would very much like to meet her again in happier circumstances.

Megan Jones, who was the *Bugle*'s Woman's Page editor, had come round to read the note and ask, 'What's he sorry for?'

'He shoved me out of the revolving door at the Grand,' said Annie. 'He's obviously got a social conscience.'

'He's obviously on the make,' remarked Megan. 'I wish men only had to look at me to start lusting after me!'

In fact Annie knew that she walked on eggshells in

some of her relationships. Women were quick to resent her and men were taken with her on sight, without having more than the sketchiest idea what she was like beneath the luminous skin. It was not instant rapport so much as instant drawbacks.

Last night's date with Huw had run maddeningly true to form. She had started going out with him a few days after that first meeting. He was a businessman in a small family engineering firm, he was cheerful and considerate, and her parents took to him.

Taking a new man home was always a little awkward for Annie because, although the men didn't know it, her mother and father were waiting for her to find a husband. Annie would marry, of course, but they wanted to see her settled. They worried about her being left alone when they died, because neither of them believed she could survive without a protector.

Huw Sanders might have fitted the bill. They had liked him and were quite happy when she was out with him. 'We know you're safe with Huw, dear,' her mother had said, and within weeks Huw was dropping hints about marriage, which Annie was not taking up. He was nearing thirty and ready to settle down, and he was enraptured with her. Wherever he took her he felt that other men were envying him, and at first it flattered him when everyone seemed to take a second look at Annie, but one evening a haircrack appeared in the relationship.

It was no surprise to her. She recognised it if Huw didn't. They were at a party. The editor of the *Bugle* was about to retire and he and his wife were holding a party for the staff. All Annie's colleagues were there, along with wives and husbands and friends. She was in a scarlet silk dress, with a white jagged-edged Peter Pan collar, and scarlet sandals, which would have made her conspicuous even if she had been plain.

It was early May and flowering cherry trees, in a

froth of pink, and crab-apple trees in muted mulberry, edged the lawn, petals drifting down like confetti when a breeze stirred the branches.

Annie was having a lovely time chatting and joking. Huw was here as her guest, and he seemed to be enjoying himself. But when she looked across at him at the other end of the lawn and one of the sports writers had his hand on her shoulder, and she was laughing, she saw Huw was not amused.

She saw his face tightening, and the way suspicion was making his eyes sharp and narrow, and her heart sank.

Here we go again, she thought, because it was a repeating pattern. Sometimes it seemed that she was never going to have the time to fall in love. She was fond of Huw, as she had been fond of others before him.

After that party Huw was less happy about her job. Until then he had been quite appreciative about it, reading her stories, asking about her day when they met at night. But after meeting the staff of the *Bugle* he had realised how many men there were compared to the women. When Annie worked late he began questioning her on who else was working.

If she could have told him she loved him it might have reassured him, and if he had not turned too possessive too soon she might have done. But last night she had sat by Huw in the Priory Wine Bar and felt that he would find fault with whatever she did or said. It was a sultry night, the tables were full, and the air-conditioning did not seem to be working. Tomorrow the new editor took over the *Bugle*. Adam Corbett was a name. Huw had heard of him, almost everybody had, so they talked about that a little, and Annie said she would be sorry to be losing the old editor. Adam Corbett was a different breed, and the staff were rather apprehensive.

'You'll be all right,' Huw had said. 'All you'll have to do is smile at him.'

Annie's smiles had smoothed her way from time to time, but this was no compliment, more a suggestion of the casting couch, and she snapped, 'If I wasn't good at my job I wouldn't be doing it.'

'Mmm,' said Huw.

A man at the next table could hardly take his eyes off her. He was florid-faced with greying hair and a curling moustache; she half smiled, catching him staring, and Huw glared, 'Do you know him?'

'No.'

'I wish you wouldn't smile at strangers.'

After that she tried to keep her gaze confined to him and the food and to be as unprovocative as possible. She did not want a row here. It was no use telling men that they didn't own her, because they immediately denied acting as though they did, and when a relationship reached the stage where she was scared to be spontaneous there was no life left in it.

'I'm not good for you,' she would say when they were in a less public place, 'and goodness knows, you're not doing me much good either.'

There was always friction now when they were together. She was probably giving him an ulcer, and he was making her feel like somebody being slowly bricked up in a wall. They shared a bottle of wine and a seafood platter, but the atmosphere was oppressively humid. Her dress was sticking to her and she blew down her neck; somebody passing with a tray of drinks gave a wolf whistle, and Huw exploded, 'This place is like a bear pit!'

He had a flat in a modern development, it would be cooler there. The crush in here was getting worse. Tonight it was so packed that they had to elbow their way to the stairs, and then up to the door to the car park.

Outside Huw asked, 'Do you actually like this place?'

'The food was all right.'

'What can you do with a seafood platter?' He plonked himself sulkily behind the wheel and Annie thought, I could tell you what to do with it. Huw felt the heat, he was sweating profusely, and he seemed to be blaming her for his discomfort.

'So we picked somewhere where trade's looking up,' she said. 'Good for them.'

She wound down the window, and as the car gathered speed the wind lifted her hair and cooled her skin, and she promised herself a cold shower as soon as she got home. She wouldn't relax until then. She couldn't relax with Huw these days; all the easiness had gone from their relationship, and tonight had been another flop. Her nerves were jumping, and when he parked the car in his parking lot and put a warm hand under her elbow to lead her into the flat block she moved away from his touch and began to chatter about the décor in the foyer, 'I like this yellow—it's a nice cheery colour.'

She hoped he wasn't going to start lecturing her when they got up there, because she knew she was a disappointment and the relationship was dead and nothing was going to revive it, so what was the use of holding an inquest? She would take a cup of coffee if he offered her one, and say quite soon that she thought she should be getting home.

He went to the fridge, took out a bottle of Muscadet and uncorked it. It would be cold, but Annie had had enough wine, and if he was driving her home so had he. She said, 'I'd rather have a cup of tea.'

'I know what you want.' He filled two glasses and carried them to a table, and he didn't know at all what she wanted. She would like to go home right now and get out of this sticky dress and wash her hair and lie between sheets. But as she started to speak Huw grabbed her and kissed her, his mouth soft and warm, his soft warm fingers sliding the dress off her shoulders.

She felt no leap of the senses, nor was she soothed or comforted, just indignant that he could claim intimacy when they were so nearly back to being strangers, and then ask, puzzled, 'What's the matter?'

'We're getting on each other's nerves.' There was plenty of proof of that. 'You're not happy with me. Most of the time I irritate you to death.'

'I'm happy with you now.' He was running his hands over her, and she felt like a cat being stroked the wrong way, ready to spit and scratch.

'It's not enough,' she said.

'It's more than enough,' he contradicted her firmly. Most of the time he didn't even like her. This might be enough for him, but it made her stomach churn. 'This is what matters,' he said, 'that when we're alone together I want you.'

He wasn't even considering whether she wanted him too. 'No,' she started to say, but he pressed her back on to the couch, his considerable weight nearly suffocating her, and she thrust up with fists and knees, gasping for air. More by luck than judgment she hit where it hurt, jerking him off balance so that he fell off the couch still clutching her, and they rolled over and over on the carpet in an undignified and ridiculous struggle.

Huw got up, scowling down at her, and she sprang to her feet, hair over her eyes. Her dress was torn open, falling off her shoulders so that she looked like a gypsy temptress from an early movie, teeth bared because the breath had been squashed out of her, hot angry colour in her cheeks, glaring back at him, and he was shaken.

Annie was the most fanciable girl he had ever met, but he had never lost his head like this before. Suppose she started screaming, accusing him of attacking her? 'I'll take you home,' he said, breathing hard.

'You can get——' Annie didn't finish that because

she had just seen the state of her dress. Her home was about five miles away and she might find a taxi, but there were still folk in the streets, and even pinned this would be conspicuous. Besides, she might not get a taxi on a Sunday night. So she said, 'You can get me a pin.'

Huw went to the dressing table drawer in his bedroom, stopping to straighten his collar and comb his hair. Tidied up he felt better, telling himself that he had not behaved badly. On the contrary, he had shown exceptional self-control.

He brought her a large safety pin and handed it over without a word, and she pulled the rip together to cover as much as possible. 'And now,' she said, 'I'd like to go home.'

It would have been a relief if he had said something on the way, even, 'Well, that's that, then,' which it assuredly was. Or turned on the radio. She ran through little speeches in her head, 'What makes you think you're the kind of lover to blow the mind so that you can be boorish as hell five minutes before and get away with it? . . . *You're* huffy? *You've* had a bad night? Well, it's hardly been a load of laughs for me . . .'

In the end she said nothing until the end of her road, when she asked him to, 'Please put me down here. I'll walk the rest of the way, I'd rather get into the house quietly.'

He drew up well before her house in the tree-lined avenue. Night was falling and there was no one about. 'Goodbye,' said Annie, 'and now perhaps you'll believe that I'm not your type and you'd be better off without me,' and she half smiled because it was like addressing a dummy with a bad-tempered face, but the smile didn't break Huw's silence, it just deepened his scowl, so she turned the key as quietly as she could, and pushed the front door open just wide enough to slip through.

The television was on. Voices and background music filled the hall. Her mother would not admit to hearing less sharp than it was, but the television sound got turned up louder these days, and Annie tiptoed down the hall and up the stairs.

She didn't switch on the light in her bedroom. There was light from outside yet, and with her door open a crack enough illumination filtered in from the hall for her to undress by. She rolled up her dress and hid it at the back of a drawer. She would get rid of that as soon as she could smuggle it out of the house. She removed her make-up with lotion and decided not to risk the bathroom.

She would rather not face them tonight. Running water and flushing cisterns would advertise that she was home, and then she would have to explain why she had come up here without even looking into the lounge.

She heard her parents moving around downstairs, and soon she heard them coming up and wondering what time she would be in tonight. They were talking about Huw, as they came upstairs and past her room. About his financial eligibility in a family firm that was ticking over nicely. 'He's a substantial young man,' mused Catrin, 'Good solid stock,' and Annie pushed her face into the pillow to stifle a yelp of laughter.

Huw was substantial all right. Twelve stone odd landing on top of her. But not so solid. When she was pummelling against him it was like fighting a load of nutty slack. That would make Megan smile. Annie could tell a funny story about her scuffle, but even while she was thinking that she caught herself sighing.

She didn't find it as easy as usual to fall asleep, and when her little alarm clock woke her, followed immediately by her mother's first call of the morning, 'Annie, it's half past seven!' she answered 'I'm awake,' and then lay staring at the ceiling.

Rocky wouldn't be sitting in the editor's chair this morning, and that was depressing. A stranger would be there—a new boss, an unknown quantity. Adam

Corbett was coming back to his roots, because he had begun his career as a trainee reporter on the *Bugle*. At twenty he went on holiday and the day after he arrived in a third world state he walked into the uprising and all hell was let loose. Young Corbett, the best junior the *Bugle* had ever had, didn't miss a trick. He sent back despatches: straight reporting that brought every scene to life, meetings with leaders and rank and file, and every interview a winner.

Annie had been a child at the time; she had never met him, but she still remembered the sensation it had caused.

Afterwards he never looked back. The *Bugle* was part of a national group. Adam Corbett returned from that working holiday as a staff reporter on the London daily, and if anybody thought that it was just a lucky break that time that he got the front page story without getting shot they were wrong, because he went on doing it.

In recent years he had freelanced, always where the action was until his luck almost ran out earlier in the year. He was the only survivor in an armoured truck that ran over a landmine on a mountain pass. But the wounds healed, he was walking with a limp, and he was coming back to edit his old newspaper.

This had come as a shock to the staff. Even a slowed-down Adam Corbett could be dynamite, and although it was rumoured he was only convalescing here he might turn awkward if his staff failed to reach his probably impossible standards.

Her father drove her to work this morning, as he had always done until his retirement. By then she had an ancient Triumph Vitesse of her own that got her to and fro more or less but was now clapped out. Annie had a soft spot for her car, and motor mechanics with a soft spot for her had done wonders in maintaining it over the last two years. But her mother was nagging, and her father was offering to help her buy a reliable little second-hand, and this morning when she turned the ignition key there had been nothing. Not even the faintest catch, although she did all the right things before she finally gave up and climbed out.

That wasted ten minutes, and at the end of it her father had to drive her in. 'How was Huw?' he asked her as they came out of the avenue and joined the busier road.

'Well——' she began, drawling it, so that he gave her a knowing look and said,

'I thought you sounded as if you were going off him. Your mother won't like that.'

'You know how it is,' said Annie. 'Some people you do go off.' She didn't want to go on discussing Huw, so she said, 'It isn't going to be the same without Rocky,' and that diverted her father's attention, and they talked about the office and Rocky and about Adam Corbett.

Her father remembered him well. 'If he does remember me,' he said, 'tell him I'd like to see him again.'

'First chance I get,' Annie promised.

They were on the outskirts of town now and the traffic was at a standstill. Roadworks were causing a bottleneck and she was getting later all the time. She bit her lip, checking her watch, deciding, 'I'd better get out and cut through the alleys.'

'Give me a ring if you want collecting.' She opened the door and hopped out, calling, 'Not to worry, I'll get a lift.'

It should have been quicker on foot, but as she hurried down a narrow passageway the slim heel of her sandal caught between the flagstones and snapped neatly in two. She lurched and stood, closed her eyes and swore. This was well on the way to being one of those days when the stars have it in for you.

She looked up and caught the expression on the face of a middle-aged woman with pink-rinsed hair, who was arranging a matching turquoise-blue handbag, scarf and belt in a small bay window. This was the back entrance to the town's most exclusive boutique, and the woman had a gleeful smirk. Meeting Annie's eyes, she changed it to a tight-lipped smile, and Annie smiled back and knew that her mishap had gone down well with Mrs Lloyd Williams, who had told all her friends three years ago, 'I shall never forgive Anna for what she did to my boy.' She probably never would, although it should have been water under the bridge by now and her 'boy' had suffered no lasting damage.

Even when things were going well Mrs Lloyd Williams' beady eyes, darting ill will, could make Annie sigh. This morning she almost mouthed, 'You too,' because she was feeling hot and cross; but she managed to keep her smile steady for a moment before hobbling away to buy the first sandals she could find in her size and price range.

After that she ran the rest of the way to work and dashed into the entrance to the *Bugle* as one of the photographers stepped into the lift. 'Hold it!' she yelled, and dived after him through the closing doors. On the way up to the editorial floor she explained what had happened to her. 'My poor old banger wouldn't start and there's a traffic hold-up, so my father dropped me off, and then I broke my heel in the cobbles and I had to go and fork out for another pair of shoes, and it's five more days till pay-day.'

'I'll buy the bit about buying the new shoes,' said Charlie, tapping the box under her arm that contained her old sandals, as they walked out of the lift.

Directly opposite was the editor's office. Glyn Rees, deputy editor, was coming through the door, with the man who had to be Adam Corbett because he was walking with a stick and a slight limp. To Annie he seemed incredibly tall, dwarfing Glyn. 'Nobody told me you were seven foot high,' she said.

Six foot two or three, probably. Broad-shouldered but lean, in a well cut suit. She had seen him on television, the occasional photograph in newspapers and magazines. His features were regular, hard, clean-cut and unsmiling. He looked through her with no reaction at all, as though she was invisible, and she said, 'I'm Annie Bennett.'

It came out as though she expected him to recognise her, which of course he wouldn't, but she felt a need to stress her identity.

Glyn was ruddy-faced and well built, a cheerful outgoing man, but the masculinity of Adam Corbett was infinitely more forceful. Glyn said kindly, 'Annie is one of our brightest young reporters as well as being the prettiest,' and Adam Corbett said, 'How do you do.'

Just that, moving on as he spoke and Annie gulped because her throat was closing as though someone had their hands around it, then she turned to Charlie.

Charlie Mann was the male heart-throb around here, with an earned reputation as a womaniser, but most of the time he amused Annie. It was the swagger, the knowing glint in his eye, that made her smile. He thought he was a helluva lad, but he had never made Annie's mouth go dry, and her throat hurt, and the muscles in her stomach clench like this. Nobody had. It was an alien sensation and not a pleasant one.

The two men walking down the corridor stopped when Glyn opened a door, and Adam Corbett turned and looked back. And her heart began to thud, making the blood roar in her ears, and incredulously she recognised the sensation as fear that was only a hair's breadth from panic.

CHAPTER TWO

UNDER her delicate prettiness Annie was a tough young lady, and she told herself, 'Don't be fanciful. What's there to be afraid of?'

'There's a turn-up for the book,' said Charlie. 'A man who doesn't think you're cute as a button.' He went on grinning up the spiral iron staircase that led to the flat roof and the photographic department, and Annie headed towards her own room. She hadn't needed Charlie to tell her what kind of impression she had made on Adam Corbett. None at all. Zero. Complete uninterest, and it wasn't fear that had gripped her a moment ago, it was pique, because she was not used to being ignored. And who the hell did he think he was anyway? Just a journalist who got the breaks, and that hardly made him Tolstoy.

There were three desks in Annie's office: her own, Megan's, and the features editor's. The only sign of the features editor at the moment was a lingering odour of pungent tobacco, and Megan was glancing through an article that had arrived in the morning post. She took another look at Annie. 'You're looking rather flushed. Everything all right?'

Annie was supposed to be in the office for nine, but her first job this morning was at ten. She was in plenty of time for that, but she was hot because she had been hurrying, and she could have told Megan about the car and the snapped heel. Instead she asked, 'Have you seen the new boss? He fancies himself, doesn't he?'

'*I* fancy him,' said Megan promptly.

'You do?' Megan was no doormat, so her first

meeting with Adam Corbett must have been more fun than Annie's.

'I like a chap with presence,' said Megan. 'He had us all in the reporters' room and nobody even shuffled, although he talked for a few minutes, saying he was glad to be here and he was sure we'd all work well together, and then he said a personal hello to everybody.'

So Annie had missed the official 'take-over', and hearing Charlie as they walked out of the lift Adam Corbett probably thought she had done a little shopping on her way to work, but that was no crime. 'Well, he didn't say hello to me,' she said tartly. 'He looked straight through me. I don't think I'm going to like him. He might be convalescing, but he doesn't look like a sick man to me. I shouldn't care to come up against him.'

'Funny you should say that,' said Megan. 'I wouldn't mind coming up against him anywhere.'

'You like him,' shrugged Annie, 'you can have him. Anyhow, I'm off men this morning. I had a right do with Huw last night. It ended up with a fight on the hearthrug.'

Megan burst out laughing. 'Sounds fun!'

Annie had a plum assignment this morning, interviewing a rock star born in the valleys who was here for the opening of a new nightclub. Jud Dane's records usually got into the charts and he appeared fairly regularly on television. Posters had been up for ages, and this Friday there would be an article by Annie, who was almost a fan and was quite looking forward to meeting him.

She had gone through his file in the office library. He was certainly a dish, bronzed and husky, photographed with stunning starlets and ex-wives, a sort of jet-set Charlie. The grin was the same, a pair of Romeos giving the girls a treat.

It was not often a genuine celebrity came Annie's way. Her stories were mostly about ordinary people who were making local news, and after Jud Dan's fortnight had launched 'Merlin's Cave' the cabaret artists might not be such topliners. He was the star attraction for starters, and she set off for the club hoping that the jinx that had dogged her morning so far had worn itself out.

The club had once been a Bingo hall and now had a new façade of dark brown and gold, proclaiming 'Merlin's Cave' in fluorescent green. The front, with its 'Jud Dane, here tonight,' signs, was locked, but as Annie rang the bell the side door was opened by a harassed-looking man she recognised as the manager.

'Ah, Miss Bennett,' he said. 'Come in, come in.' She could hear the throbbing sexy voice in Jud Dane's latest song, backed by strings, drums, piano, as she followed the manager down the corridor through a door that led into the club.

'He's fantastic, isn't he?'

A balcony had been converted into a restaurant. Here, downstairs, tables edged a small dance floor, and on the stage Jud and his group were rehearsing their act. Annie was just in time to catch the end of it. She sat down at a table and wished she had come sooner.

Jud was pacing up and down as he sang, wearing tight-fitting jeans, shirtless, gold medallions glinting in the dark curling hair of his chest.

According to legend Merlin of Camelot was a Welsh wizard, and still sleeping somewhere near here in an enchanted cave, until the time came when all the knights of the Round Table would ride out again to save the world. Murals of medieval knights and ladies and castles covered the walls, with a brooding study of Merlin looking like a Walt Disney character.

Annie sat watching the stage, elbows on the table, chin on laced fingers. The group had all noticed when the manager had brought her in and taken her to a central table, and now Jud Dane swaggered down the small sloping runway to sing the last few throbbing words to her.

'That was lovely,' she said, as the music died away.

'Lovely,' he echoed. He kissed her fingertips, and went on holding her hand and looking into her face. 'You're in show business yourself, of course?'

'No.'

'You should be, little girl. You're very beautiful.'

'This is Anna Bennett,' said the manager. 'Local press.'

Jud Dane registered exaggerated amazement. 'Impossible! She's much too pretty to be a journalist.'

That kind of remark always meant you looked too dumb, but Annie thanked him, smiling, and asked, 'May I ask you a few questions?'

'Nothing I'd like better. Well,' he leered, just like Charlie, 'I *can* think of something nicer, of course—but yes, you can ask your questions. Let's go and make ourselves comfortable.'

His dressing room was big enough for changing costumes and applying theatrical make-up and, with a divan bed along one wall, probably for anything else he had in mind. He stood in front of the mirror, flexing his shoulder blades as though he was relaxing the tension of the rehearsal and, Annie suspected, giving her the chance to admire his muscles. It might have been a turn-on, if it hadn't been such a show-off that she was tempted to give him a round of applause.

Instead she said the usual complimentary things about his music, settling herself on a stool with her notebook open and ballpoint pen poised; while Jud Dane stood, arms folded, legs apart, looking her up and down, all his gold medallions rising and falling with his heavy breathing.

'Mr Dane,' she began.

'Jud. Everybody calls me Jud.' He flung his arms wide, as though embracing them all, and Annie was glad to see him fold them again because she had to get her story first, and then she could say, 'Thank you very much and goodbye,' if he tried embracing her.

'Jud,' she said, 'now you're right at the top of your profession,' he wasn't exactly at the very top, but he took the compliment with a smirk, 'have you any other ambitions? Any exciting plans for the future?'

'Only to find happiness. True love. The right woman.'

'Tell me about her,' said Annie. 'And tell me about yourself.'

He talked about himself first, and it had all been told before. His career had taken off when he cut his first disc and changed his name from Dai Griffith to Jud Dane. He talked about his songs and his travels and then about love, leering at Annie as though he could have gobbled her up.

He was a great lover, he was in no doubt about that. Passionate, but generous. 'I have so much to give that sometimes I give too much, but nothing matters more than love, not even music. Don't you agree?'

'I can't really make comparisons,' said Annie. 'I'm not a musician.'

'We could make music together.' Close up the little lines of dissipation showed, although the face was so smooth that you suspected a tuck here and there, and his teeth were so perfect they had to be capped. He thought he was bowling her over. She had her feet tucked under the bar of the stool, but as he began to move towards her she slipped them out so that she could stand up quickly and get out.

'Have you ever had a real man, little girl?' he asked, in a husky, infinitely suggestive voice, and as she had just decided there was a lot about him that was phoney she nearly grinned.

'I must be on my way,' she said. 'I've a very tight schedule today.'

'I'll see you again?'

'You're here for a fortnight, so who knows?' She didn't want to antagonise him. This way he thought she was overwhelmed by his fame and his sex appeal. She thanked him for the interview and closed her notebook.

'Anything else you need. I'm staying at the Grand, in a nice little suite, all on my own.'

'If I can't read my notes I'll be in touch.'

She wondered if he considered that a promise, because he went on smiling, and his fingers were massaging her shoulder as she opened the door and stepped into the corridor.

She finished the article before she went out to lunch, and she thought it was a reasonable piece. She left out the pass, but told her readers about Jud Dane's dream girl, and described him as being sexy and charming and talented. And although she wouldn't be seeing him again the pass had been a compliment, and she hoped the show went well and the new nightclub was lucky.

Annie and Megan ate at a salad bar, after Megan had shopped for the evening meal and Annie had taken her sandals in for repair. Forking down her cottage cheese, Annie told Megan about Jud Dane suggesting they made music together.

They were eating outside in the little patio, a table for two against the whitewashed wall hung with brilliant baskets of hanging fuchsias, and Annie mimicked the condescending leeriness of, 'Have you ever had a real man, little girl?' and had Megan laughing.

'I should think the tan was genuine,' said Annie. 'He'd just come back from Spain, but close-up he looks pretty much a made-over job.'

'You didn't stay to find out?'

'You're kidding!'

Almost as soon as they got back to the office the

phone rang on Megan's desk. 'Yes, O.K.,' she said, and replacing it she told Annie, 'Adam Corbett wants to see you.'

'Now?'

'Right now.'

Annie shrugged, looking blank and feeling uneasy. She didn't want to see him, and yet there was no reason why she should get this frisson of—not fear, no, more an extra alertness as though a warning bell was ringing.

She walked slowly along the corridor, remembering that Megan had said Adam had greeted them all personally this morning, so he obviously did intend getting to know his staff. He had probably been preoccupied when he and Glyn met her, and if he was half way amiable now she would pass on her father's message and invitation.

Reaching his door, she found herself running her tongue between her lips. They felt dry and stiff, and as she knocked the door she made them smile. It wasn't that easy to get it right so that she looked relaxed, not grinning like a clown. 'Come in,' he called.

He was behind Rocky's desk that had always been covered with papers. This morning the desk was almost bare. The same reference books were on the shelves, the same old prints of the castles of Wales on the walls, but the man in the chair changed everything. He was looking up when Annie walked in, and the smile set on her lips.

She went towards him, unable to look away. When she was within a step of the desk she stopped and swallowed and said, 'You sent for me?' and she could swear perspiration was breaking out on her forehead.

It looked like her copy in front of him. He lifted the pages, scanning as he turned them. His hands were brown and thin and almost certainly strong. No rings. A watch. Annie looked at the watch and felt she could hear it ticking. If it wasn't the watch it was a pulse in her temples.

His voice was quiet, almost drawling. He said, 'When Glyn Rees said you were one of our brightest reporters he can't have been referring to your work.'

It *was* her story he was reading, and she croaked, 'What's wrong with it? Bearing in mind that the *Bugle* is a small-town paper and we may not all be up to your kind of journalism.'

He wasn't rising to that. She couldn't crack his calm. She was suddenly sure that if she had hit him across the face he wouldn't have turned a hair.

He laid a flat hand on the typewritten pages and told her, 'This is lazy writing. You've followed nothing through. He's looking for true love, he says—well, he's been married three times, so how did his ex-wives fall short? Or maybe he did. And the girl-friends. Get a few more quotes. Ask some of them their opinion of him, and get some bite into it. This sounds as if his P.R.O. wrote it.'

Her face flamed. She felt like a schoolgirl with an essay that had been marked, 'Weak. Must do better.'

'All right?' The lecture was over and he didn't expect her to argue. He expected her to take this back and start again.

'You're the editor,' she shrugged. 'You can pull rank any time you please.'

Adam Corbett smiled then, but not the way men usually smiled at her. 'Now I heard you were the privileged one around here. And don't stand there, get on with it.'

'Yes, *sir*!'

'Read that,' Annie said to Megan, handing her the rejected article. Megan read and said, 'Yes?'

'What would you say was wrong with it?'

'Nothing. Super-stud looking for love. Aren't they all?'

'He,' Annie jerked her head towards the corridor because she couldn't trust herself to say Adam

Corbett's name, 'wants a rewrite, because this is lazy stuff with nothing followed through. He wants me to ask some of super-stud's exes how *he* measures up.'

'Hey, yes!' Megan thought it was a good idea. 'You might get something interesting, there were enough of them.'

'And another thing, he said he'd heard I was the privileged one around here. What do you think he meant by that?'

'Search me,' said Megan. 'Mind you, you have always been lucky.'

Annie couldn't deny that, although she had a premonition that so long as Adam Corbett was just along the corridor the easy times were over, and she sat down at her desk, seething.

She was covering a meeting at the town hall this afternoon, and she should have been able to stroll along there with plenty of time in hand. Now she had to start making a list of Jud Dane's lovers and begin thinking how she might contact them.

Almost everyone at the town hall knew Annie. She was greeted with smiles, from the girl in Reception to the members of the Planning Committee, and she sat down on the press bench while just below the case was argued for turning what had been a launderette in the high street into a Chinese takeaway.

She took shorthand notes and tried to keep her mind off Adam Corbett. He was probably right about her Jud Dane story. He had probably never interviewed anybody without digging out more than they meant to tell. Something that read like a public relations handout must be an awful bore to him. Rocky would have thought it was a nice little story, but Rocky never stirred up trouble. Rocky was a cautious soul, but Adam Corbett, she felt, was afraid of nobody.

He was like the storm centre, so dangerous that getting near him could be deadly. Not that Annie would be trying to get near. She wouldn't know how to start. That old trick, if someone made you feel inferior, of imagining them naked and vulnerable didn't work either. She could look across this room and visualise the ladies and gentlemen of the planning committee all baby-pink and naked.

That made her smile, and she ducked her head because the Chinese takeaway was no laughing matter, the members who were against it were getting heated. But she could only imagine Adam Corbett as she had seen him this morning, in the charcoal grey well-cut suit. A man with unassailable barriers.

One of the younger councillors caught her eye and winked at her, and she smiled back and thought, Whether I like it or not he's a brilliant journalist and I'd be a fool not to learn as much as I can from him.

She would work late tonight, and tomorrow she would set about finding someone who had something lively to say about Jud Dane. She would show Adam Corbett that she was a real reporter, not the empty-headed glamour-puss he had her marked down as, and then maybe she would find that he was human after all.

Megan's husband Barry, who taught English at the local comprehensive and wrote poetry in Welsh in his spare time, always collected her from work. He was in the office when Annie got back, a stocky cheerful man, sitting on the edge of his wife's desk.

John Hogan, the features editor, was puffing his foul pipe and it was coming round to half five. Megan's shopping basket was on her desk. They were chatting away the last few minutes before they all went home, and as Annie walked in Barry chuckled and said, 'It's as well I'm not a jealous man.'

'Not you,' Annie smiled. 'And what's brought this on?'

'The way she's carrying on about your new boss,' said Barry. 'She says he's dead sexy.'

'Oh he *is*,' said Megan, and Annie opened her mouth to say, 'Well, I don't think so,' then closed it. 'Do you want a lift?' Barry asked her.

'Thanks, but I've got these notes to type out.'

She might blow her budget by taking a taxi when she was through, and she got down to work on her shorthand report of the planning meeting—where the takeaway had been turned down; and then she rang the Grand Hotel to ask if Jud Dane would speak to Anna Bennett of the *Bugle*.

She didn't want another personal interview, it might get too personal, if it was possible to contact him by phone; and she was relieved a few moments later to hear him say, 'Hello there.'

'Sorry to bother you,' she began.

'I was expecting you. Come on up.' He must be answering the phone in his suite, presuming she was down in the lobby, but his confidence was misplaced.

'I'm in the office,' she told him. 'It was a little talk I wanted.'

'A *talk*?'

'About what you were telling me, about your search for the one woman. I was wondering what happened with the others. You've had three wives, what went wrong there?'

'You don't need to worry about them,' he said.

'I don't?'

'I could tell you,' and he proceeded to tell her how his wives had treated him and how much they had cost him. Then he laughed off the girls whose names had been linked with his. 'There's nobody, little girl,' he said, his voice husky with self-pity. 'I'm a very lonely man. And when I saw you sitting there this morning, looking like a breath of spring, I thought—but this could be her, I could have found my soulmate.'

'Really?' said Annie sweetly, certain that souls were the last thing on Mr Dane's mind. 'Well, it has been nice talking to you, and good luck for tonight.'

'You could make it a night to remember for both of us.' He was putting all the suggestive promise he could into that, and she pulled a face as she hung up.

There were still a few people in the building, but it was emptying rapidly as she made her way to the lift and the top of the stairs. The door of the editor's room was closed, and she wondered if Adam Corbett was still in there and how he would spend his evening. If he would eat alone, he was staying at the local hotel, or with friends. And as she walked down the stairs she wondered why she kept thinking about him, because all day he had hardly been out of her mind.

Annie let herself into the house and called, 'I'm home!'

'In the kitchen!' her mother called back. 'Your father went to meet you.'

'I took a taxi. I'll be right down, I'm just going to have a wash.'

She washed, then changed into a clean fresh cotton blouse and skirt, as the sweltering weather had stained the low-cut sleeveless dress she had worn all day, and she was brushing her hair when her mother came in, asking, 'Had a nice day, dear?'

'Not bad.'

Later she would tell them about Adam Corbett, but not that he had more or less said that she was a rotten journalist, because they were proud of her cleverness. And about Jud Dane, but not that he had marked her down as easy. That would have horrified and worried them sick.

Her mother closed the door with an embarrassed little laugh and began, 'I'm rather worried. Well, there is something I want to ask you.'

Annie stopped brushing her hair and twisted round on her stool as her mother said in a rush of words, 'I did some washing this afternoon and I looked to see if there was anything you might have forgotten to put into the linen basket, and in that drawer,' she gestured towards the chest of drawers, 'I found the frock you were wearing when you went out with Huw last night.'

The one that was ripped. If she had not led such a sheltered life she might have presumed unbridled, but not necessarily unwelcome, passion and said nothing at all. But Catrin looked deeply troubled, so Annie explained, 'Things got a little rough.'

'Not *Huw*? You don't mean *Huw* tore your dress?'

'Well, yes.'

'But why—? I mean——'

'Because,' said Annie gently, 'we're not getting along too well any more. Last night I told him I thought we should finish, and we had a sort of skirmish.'

Catrin closed her eyes as though shutting out a scene too horrific to contemplate. 'He didn't—? He never—?' She could hardly frame the word in her mind, much less say it. She knew that girls did get treated roughly, but not Annie. All the same, the thought of Huw—who was such a nice young man—forcing himself on Annie made her quite faint with shock.

'Of course not,' said Annie, and she smiled as though there had never been the slightest danger.

Her mother was obviously desperate to be reassured, and Annie knew that ever since she unrolled that dress just after lunch she would have been telling herself there had to be a harmless explanation. Now Annie was insisting that no harm had been done. There had been a quarrel and Huw had grabbed her and her dress had been torn, but nobody had been hurt.

Catrin sat quietly, composing herself for a few seconds, while Annie started brushing her hair again, then she said, 'He must have lost his head. It must have been dreadful for him when you told him everything was over when he thought everything was all right, and he's so fond of you. I'm sure he was sorry about your dress.'

'Heartbroken,' Annie muttered, and her mother chided gently,

'That isn't kind. I thought you liked him.'

'I did.' Until he had stopped liking her. Continued to want her but stopped liking her. 'But it isn't working.'

'You can't treat men like this, you know,' her mother warned her. 'It isn't fair to them. I'm sure it's fun to flirt, but it isn't always kind, and it must be frightening if a man loses his temper.'

No man had ever lost his temper with Catrin, not her father nor her husband, and there had been no other man in her life. 'I don't suppose anything like this has happened before,' Catrin went on, and Annie, who could have told her with honesty, 'So often I've lost count, I've been fighting them off for years,' said, 'Well . . .' and her mother said, 'I'm sure it hasn't, and I'm sure it's been a warning to you. We won't say anything to your father—he'd be very angry and he mustn't be upset.'

'Of course we won't,' said Annie, and her mother sighed regretfully,

'Oh, if only you'd married David!'

'Not that again!' Annie begged.

'I could have had a grandchild by now. You could have been settled in your own home. Such a pretty little house—I still can't bear to walk by it.'

'I could have been separated, divorced,' Annie said quietly. 'Going through with it would have been the mistake.'

'He was a nice young man.'

'Still is, I hope,' Annie said flippantly. 'I didn't actually murder him,' and her mother sighed again and went out of the room looking martyred. 'Oh hell!' muttered Annie to her reflection in the mirror.

It was all of three years ago, but she still felt guilty. She was nineteen, but even then her parents were anxious to see her married, and everything was planned for a June wedding. The invitations were out, and

Annie had had her last fitting for her wedding dress when she came to her senses.

That was exactly what had happened. She saw sense, instead of the stars that had been in her eyes ever since David had put the sapphire and diamond ring on her finger and kissed her and said, 'Now you're mine, aren't you?'

'I suppose I am,' she'd agreed, and everyone had been thrilled. Her mother and David's mother had organised everything so that within two months every detail of the wedding was planned, a honeymoon in the Greek islands was booked, and the fathers had paid the deposit on a house as their combined gift.

The house was almost furnished with other wedding presents, and then Annie realised that she couldn't marry him. When she first said, 'I can't go through with it,' it was put down to pre-wedding nerves and everyone tried to laugh it off. David wouldn't listen at first. 'Nothing to it,' he kept reassuring her, as though they were talking about the wedding ceremony, not the lifetime that would follow; and even when he held the ring in his hand he went back into the house to tell her parents, 'Annie's panicking.'

'I'm so sorry,' she told everybody. David. His parents. Her parents. Their friends. She was racked with guilt, hating herself but facing the stark truth that she was not ready for marriage and that she had let herself be pressured and rushed into this situation.

She never doubted that she had been right to draw back, it would have been a disaster for both of them, but she was terribly sorry about all the trouble she had caused, and although David had married another girl in just over a year he had moved away from here, and his mother had never forgiven Annie.

Annie's mother only harked back in times of great stress. When her father had his heart attack her mother had sobbed, 'Oh, why didn't you marry David? I shan't last long after your father, and then you'll be all alone.' And now that Annie had finished with Huw her mother would be casting around for some other nice and eligible man.

'Oh, *hell!*' Annie said again. She heard her father's car turn into the drive, she should have phoned and said she was taking a taxi, she must have just missed him. She spent a few minutes getting out the clothes she would wear tomorrow, and as she came downstairs she heard her father's voice from the lounge. Then another voice, and her father's laugh, and she went towards the open door and Adam Corbett stood up.

He *was* tall. She had recognised the deep slow voice, although she hadn't caught the words. She had been prepared for him, but when he stood up she still felt overshadowed. 'Goodness,' she said faintly. 'Hello.'

'We've got a guest,' said her father. He was still chuckling, as though he hadn't finished appreciating the joke or whatever it was that he had just been told. 'You two have met, of course.'

'We surely have,' said Annie. 'I got a taxi home—I didn't think you'd come out for me.'

'That's all right, love,' said her father, and his pride in her showed in his voice and his eyes, and she was conscious of Adam Corbett's ironic gaze. She wanted to explain that she wasn't always chauffeured around. She explained,

'My car wouldn't start this morning, so my father took me into work, and then we hit the roadworks, didn't we?' appealing to her father, who nodded, 'and,' telling her father now, 'as I was running I caught my heel and snapped it off and I had to buy another pair of shoes, so I was a good twenty minutes late getting into the office. Still,' she smiled a wide bright smile, 'I've just done an hour's overtime to make up for it.'

She was babbling like a shallow brook and he was as still as deep water, and she had better shut up, because that was the only way she could be fairly sure she would not make a fool of herself. 'A drink?' she said. 'Can I get you anything?'

'I'm just doing that,' said her father, which, as he had the whisky bottle in his hand, any fool could see. Annie was not much of a spirit drinker, but for the first time in her life she watched the amber liquid splash into the glass and was tempted to say, 'Make mine a stiff one.' But getting half stoned was no way to stay cool. 'I'll see what Mother's having,' she said, and backed out of the room.

Her mother was in the kitchen, spinning out the evening meal to include one more. Catrin was adept at that sort of thing, she could put on a hospitable welcome any time. Now she was cooking another couple of cutlets in the microwave, and chopping and mixing more salad. 'Go and talk to them', she said as Annie walked in.

'They're doing all right.'

'Go *on*, I don't need you in here.'

I don't want to go back in there, Annie thought; but it was silly to be hovering about in her own home because she felt uncomfortable with the man who was sitting on the sofa in the lounge. She poured a glass of white wine from an already opened bottle in the fridge, and another for her mother, who said, 'Put it down, dear,' and went on chopping mint.

Annie went back very quietly into the room where her father and Adam were talking about today's news. Adam had been out of international journalism for nearly six months, but he seemed to know the background to most current events, and she thought, I don't suppose he can wait to get back to where the big world-shaking things are happening.

There was still fighting in the area where his armoured truck had run over a landmine. 'We were all very shocked when we heard you'd nearly bought it,' said her father. 'You were very lucky.'

The men with him had died, and when he agreed, 'Yes, I was lucky,' Annie knew that he was remembering them.

Fate must have taken a hand there, that he was sitting where the blast threw him instead of smashing him into oblivion, and as she looked at him now he seemed more alive than anyone else she knew and a wave of thankfulness swept through Annie. She hardly knew him, she didn't particularly like him, but she found herself praying silently, 'Thank you God,' as though, if he had died that day, her own life would have been worthless.

'Ready, are we?' Catrin appeared in the doorway, smiling away Adam's apologies at his intrusion. Douglas had set off to see if Annie was still at work and returned with Adam Corbett, and Catrin had speedily laid the dining table for four, with the best cutlery. There was plenty of food now and she seated him opposite Annie and thought how distinguished he looked. He did too. Annie was thinking the same thing.

The phone rang almost as soon as they were seated, and Annie murmured, 'I'll get it,' and stepped into the hall to answer. It was a young man who had been in the wine bar last night and seen how it was between Annie and Huw, now he was ringing to ask how Annie felt about a barbecue that was being held next Saturday.

Would she go with him? he meant, and she said, 'Sorry, but I can't, thanks all the same,' and hung up before he could ask when she was free. She didn't want to start dating Robert, an opportunist who had another think coming if he was hoping to catch her on the rebound.

'Who was it, dear?' enquired her mother as Annie took her seat again.

'Robert Marsden.'

'Who?' asked her father, and Catrin explained,

'You know him, dear, he works in the post office. A sharp-featured young man.'

'The foxy one, with gingery hair?' Her father was teasing, 'What did he want?' and if Adam hadn't been here Annie would have laughed and said, 'He is foxy, isn't he? Would you go to a barbecue with a man with a foxy face?' But she didn't want to talk about her caller in front of Adam. She said,

'Oh, it was about a barbecue I can't get to anyway. Do you find the town much changed from when you lived here?'

'Not in essentials,' said Adam, and they discussed the changes. Annie was quieter than usual, but her parents blossomed in the company of their guest, who did have a sense of humour, because he could be very funny. He made them all laugh, and he asked questions that had Catrin and Douglas chatting nineteen to the dozen.

'My goodness!' cried Catrin, clapping a hand over her mouth after she had told Adam that the last guest speaker at the W.I. had been such a bore that the audience found it hard to keep their eyes open. 'I didn't mean to say that. It was very kind of her to tell us about her brass rubbings.'

There's a little thing, thought Annie, but it proves that the only way of keeping anything from him is to keep your mouth shut. I wouldn't want him questioning me if I had secrets.

Everybody was relaxed. Annie was considering her words carefully before she said anything, but it was a very successful meal, and when Adam complimented Catrin she said she loved cooking and Annie was a very good cook too.

That seemed to surprise him, and Annie said, 'Not very good, just average,' unable to stop the flood of her mother's praises until she added, 'But coffee I'm good at, I'll get the coffee,' and escaped into the kitchen.

Being praised to Adam embarrassed her because he

thought she was overrated all round, at work and at home, and when her mother followed her to say, 'We'll have it in the lounge,' Annie begged,

'I wish you wouldn't tell Adam how clever you think I am. It makes me feel such a fool.'

'But you are clever,' said her mother.

The phone rang again as they drank their coffee, and this time it was Huw. 'Well?' he demanded. 'Have you got anything to say to me?'

He was expecting an apology, he still thought she had given him a raw deal. 'Only what I said last night,' she said. 'I don't want to see you again.'

'You're spoiled—do you know that?'

'So everybody's telling me,' she said wearily, 'but I'm learning to live with it. You should try facing up to your problems some time.'

'What problems have I got?' Jealousy, possessiveness, a complete lack of sensitivity.

'Not modesty, for sure,' she snapped, and put down the phone.

When she turned she realised that she had left the door ajar, and when she went back into the lounge she knew they had all heard what she had said. Her father was chuckling, Adam's expression was wryly amused, and her mother was looking sad.

'She doesn't treat the men in her life very well,' her father said to Adam, and her mother sighed, 'I don't think it's funny. She can't go on like this for ever. I just wish she could meet a man who could handle her.'

'For heaven's sake,' muttered Annie through gritted teeth, 'you make me sound like an unbroken colt!'

'Not a bad description,' said her father. 'You've got the legs for it.' He was joking, but Catrin wasn't, and as she turned her head to look at Adam Annie's blood ran cold, because she was reading her mother's thoughts.

'You're not married, are you?' asked her mother, and searing embarrassment ran through Annie.

No way could she let him believe she was any part of this. 'She means are you looking for a wife?' She looked straight at him, her voice mocking. 'Because, as you gather, my mother is desperate to marry me off. Although it isn't a husband she wants for me so much as a minder.'

Catrin blushed painfully, on the edge of tears of humiliation. Then Adam laughed and said, 'I'm sure your minder would have his work cut out, but life would never be dull,' and the situation was defused, as simply as that.

Annie felt gauche and silly, which was probably how Adam Corbett would have described her. 'Sorry,' she apologised, 'but it has been one of those days.'

'Starting early,' he said.

He knew now why she had arrived late at work. That was one small misunderstanding cleared up, and as she sat down again Annie thought, Trying to make you see me differently could become an obsession with me. 'More coffee?' She picked up his cup.

'A man who could handle her,' her mother had just said, meaning control her; but Annie wondered how Adam would handle a woman, what his touch would be like. He and her father were talking about the garden now, with its profusion of flowers and bushes and trees framed by the french windows, colours muted by moonlight.

Annie poured black coffee, no sugar, and handed it to Adam. He took it with a word of thanks and their fingers brushed in passing, and she felt a shock run tingling up her arm so that for a moment she thought the hot coffee had splashed her.

CHAPTER THREE

ANNIE jumped up and went to the windows, opening them a fraction, although tiny moths were fluttering against the glass. That touch had been electric, she could feel it still, pins and needles in her fingers, and she knew why. It was because she had been wondering just before what Adam would be like as a lover that the fleeting brush of hands had seemed like an intimacy.

'How about a stroll round the garden?' her father suggested. He had started to tell Adam what he was doing out there, on his acre of land, since his retirement.

It was hot indoors and Annie's face was burning. Whether anyone else walked round the garden or not, she could do with some fresh air. 'I'd like that,' said Adam, and Catrin asked solicitously,

'How are you for walking?' In the reflection from the window Annie saw him getting up from his chair.

'Fine,' he said. 'Not too good at running yet.' So he wouldn't catch her if she went fast. He wouldn't be trying to catch her. Not tonight. Not ever. This was the man she couldn't have.

She went a little ahead. It was too late to see details, but the moonlight was bright enough for paths and outlines, and they had a conducted tour past the rockeries and the waterlily pond and through the rose garden.

'My wife insists that a rose has scent,' said Douglas. 'She won't have a scentless rose in the house or the garden,' and the soft night air was fragrant.

Annie hadn't turned, but she realised then that her mother had not come out with them and wondered why, because Catrin was as proud of the garden as Douglas was. They strolled arm-in-arm out here, and he always cut the first and the last rose of summer for her. In between she raided his flowerbeds, but the first and last rose were ceremoniously presented to her.

One year she had painted watercolours of a white bud, just opening, and a full-blown scarlet rose, its petals falling. They hung in gilt oval frames on the lounge wall. Catrin was a talented artist, an old loft was her studio. All her birthday and Christmas cards were originals, and friends often framed them because they were so pretty.

The garden ended in a patio backed by a high windbreaker hedge, although tonight there was no wind. Annie sat on the old stone seat and looked up to the hills. She hadn't looked towards Adam at all. Her father had done most of the talking and she had listened for Adam's few words every now and then, because he had an attractive voice, quiet and carrying.

The two men stood with their backs towards her, Adam a head taller than her father. Douglas Bennett was saying how badly the garden needed rain, sighing over the hot summer, and Annie nearly went over to put a hand through his arm and tell him the rain must be coming soon.

She took a step, but then she stopped, because she wanted to run her fingers down the dark outline of Adam's arm, over the cloth of his sleeve, or rest them on his shoulder, and she was not at all sure that she could make that seem casual. She was not fooling herself, it would not be casual. When she had thought she was falling in love, when someone she fancied had fancied her, then touching had been lovely. But this overwhelming need for contact, so that her hand seemed to reach out instinctively, was different and disturbing.

She sat down again and laced her fingers together,

and her mother's voice came floating through the night. 'Douglas, the phone!'

'Excuse me,' said Annie's father. 'Who is it?' he called back, as he made for the house.

Adam came and sat beside Annie, and she said the first thing that entered her head, as though if she sat silently he would guess how she was feeling. 'The nightclub this morning wasn't my idea of Merlin's Cave. The walls were painted all over with murals like a cartoon. Do you believe he's somewhere around here? That would be a story, wouldn't it, if a potholer fell over Merlin.'

'It would,' he agreed.

'I used to think I knew the cave. Up there.' She looked again in the direction of the hills. 'When I was very young I was exploring and I thought I heard breathing. It was a trick of the wind, of course, but I was sure for a while that I'd found the crystal cave.' She had been nine years old, but she could still remember the thrill, and the terror—because in the end she had nearly got herself buried alive trying to follow the 'breathing'. She had never told anyone. If her parents had found out she would never have been allowed to wander off alone again.

'Talking of the nightclub,' she said, 'I phoned Jud Dane and got some more quotes from him. By the end of the week the story might meet with your approval—although,' she added with a flash of mischief, 'I doubt if I will.'

'Why?' he smiled at her. 'What did you have planned?'

'Nothing in particular,' she said. 'But you're not exactly one of my fans, are you?' She had nothing planned, but she wanted his approval, she wanted him on her side. 'Honestly,' she said, 'I try. I work quite hard. I do my best, although I suppose I could do better.'

'Who couldn't? Your mother seems worried about you.'

'She need not be. I manage quite nicely on the whole.'

'They tell me you get away with murder.' The smile was still in his voice, and she demanded, 'Who tells you?'

'Most of them were happy about it.'

Annie had more friends than enemies. Mrs Lloyd Williams couldn't stand her, and there were those who thought she had it all too easy, but she had good friends and yet there was no one she would rather be with now, sitting under the moon with the perfume of roses in the air.

There were so many things she wanted to ask him. She would like to say, 'Tell me something everybody doesn't know. I've just told you about finding Merlin's cave when I was nine years old, and that was a secret. Don't you have a secret you could tell me?' He had secrets. He had that kind of face, strong and controlled. In profile, because he wasn't looking at her, just sitting beside her, and she wanted to reach up and run a fingertip down his cheek, tracing the bone of the smooth hard jawline. He was as self-contained as though he was alone, while she was longing more every minute to move into his arms.

She would have liked it very much if he had put an arm along the back of the old stone seat and around her shoulders. She would have put her head on his shoulder then and it would have been absolutely right. Most men couldn't keep their hands off her, but Adam wasn't going to touch her. This morning he had thought she was pampered and not over-bright. Now he thought she was amusing too but still dizzy. He felt no urge to get closer to her; a girl who needed a minder would hardly be his type, and what type was? she wondered.

'Tell me what kind of girl you go for.' She would have liked to say: 'I might be nearer than you think.'

She was expecting to see her father coming back. It was such a still night that they would hear his footsteps on paths and paving stones. They had heard her mother's voice clearly, but not the phone ringing, although you could usually hear the phone out here in the garden, and suddenly Annie knew it had been a ruse to get her father indoors and leave her out here with Adam.

Her mother thought that the moon and the roses were such a romantic combination that it would be like an old movie. What she hadn't considered was that Adam was too cynical to be influenced by moonlight. Or anything but his own eyes and his own judgment. If he suspected what was going on he might be amused, or he might decide that it was pathetic. A matchmaking mother, and a small town girl who fancied her chances.

She stood up, asking, 'Shall we go back?'

He reached for his stick. He didn't lean heavily on it, but it helped his balance, and stepping down the shallow step from the patio she turned to make sure he was all right, and she was the one who slipped. She stumbled heavily against him and heard the intake of breath, felt the stiffening of muscles as he steadied her, and knew that she had hurt him like hell.

'Oh, I'm *sorry*!' She swayed back, 'I should know where the step is by now. Did I hurt you?'

'No,' he said.

'I suppose you could hardly say, "Of course you did, you clumsy cow",' and he grinned, and she said, 'Please say it, I'm sure it would make you feel better.'

'Let's consider it said.'

'All right.' She wished she could have said, 'You wouldn't like a shoulder instead of that stick, would you? I'm just the right height for that.' But she knew Adam leaned on no one and that soon he would throw away the stick. She breathed deeply of the scented night air and said, because she had to say something, 'My mother paints roses. Did you notice the flower paintings?'

'Yes. They're very attractive.'

The bulk of the building that had once been stables, and was now the garage and a gardening shed with the loft over it, loomed at the back of the house. 'She has a studio up there.' Annie trotted out the information as they walked slowly back. 'My father had it fitted out for her birthday.' Catrin's sixtieth, but that was only mentioned to those who knew anyway. 'She's always painted flowers—watercolours. And my father's always been a keen gardener. In fact they're so horticulturally minded I reckon I'm lucky they didn't name me Forget-me-not.'

'I shouldn't think that was necessary,' said Adam.

That could mean she was not easily forgettable, or it could just mean she talked too much. 'I suppose Anna Bennett sounds more literary,' she said.

'Very Jane Austen.' He was either laughing with her or at her. Annie hoped it was with her, and asked, 'Do you have another name?'

'Just Adam. My parents had simple tastes.' They were both dead—she knew that.

'Well,' she said, 'Adam was enough for the first man,' and she went smiling, a few steps ahead of him, into the house.

If her father had had a phone call he was off the phone now, back in the lounge. When they walked in through the french windows he said, 'A brandy?'

'No, thank you,' said Adam, 'but if I could call a taxi.'

'I'll give you a lift.' The hotel wasn't far. Of course her father would run him back.

'I'd offer,' said Annie, 'but I can't guarantee I could get my car to start.'

'I can guarantee you wouldn't,' said her father. 'They took it away this morning.'

'And I never even asked!' She sighed dramatically. '*Not* to the knacker's yard?'

'To the garage,' he said. 'Phone them in the morning, but I don't hold out much hope.'

Her mother came into the room. 'You're not going already?' She looked at the carriage clock on the mantelpiece and stared. 'I suppose it is getting on. I hadn't realised.'

Time flies when you're having fun, thought Annie. I don't want him to go, but I'm not sure whether I'm having fun or getting more out of my depth all the time. I think I shall feel better when he's gone.

She went into the hall to say goodbye, and Adam thanked her mother and her again. He shook her mother's hand, but he didn't shake Annie's. 'I'll see you tomorrow,' he told her.

'Back to Jud Dane,' she said. I didn't mention, did I, that he offered me a night to remember if I hung around? She might have said that if her parents had not been here, because tonight had already been a night to remember. Every word Adam had said, every move he had made, was imprinted on her mind as though he *was* the first man. Or, even worse, the last.

When the front door closed she stared at it for a few seconds. 'What a charming man!' her mother was gushing. 'And your father says he's a brilliant journalist.'

'That's what they say,' said Annie. 'Was there a phone call? Did somebody want to speak to him?'

'I did,' her mother smiled. 'I thought you and Adam might like a little time on your own.'

'Please don't,' Annie begged, 'please, *please* don't!' It had been bad enough with other eligible men, but never so blatant before. 'If he's needing a wife,' she added, 'I'm sure there's one lined up.' There probably was, and the thought depressed her. She followed her mother into the kitchen, where the last few dishes were draining, and Catrin picked up the tea-towel she had dropped hearing Adam and Annie coming in from the garden. 'You were thirty-five when you got married,' Annie pointed out for the umpteenth time, and her mother replied as she always did,

'But I had your father waiting for me.' She polished a plate carefully, they had used the best china tonight. 'I knew I was never going to be lonely.'

'There are worse fates,' said Annie, and her mother sighed. 'Please,' said Annie again. 'He's my boss and I work for him, and I would rather he didn't get the impression that you're running a marriage bureau here with just me on the books.'

Catrin sighed and said, 'I know he's your boss at work, and I wish you could meet a man who was your boss out of work, who would make you behave yourself.'

There was nothing else to do down here. The washing up was tidied away. Annie kissed her mother and said, 'I don't like the sound of that, it doesn't sound much fun.'

'Why won't you be serious?' sighed Catrin. 'We only want what's best for you.'

She only wanted happiness for Annie, Annie knew, but with this man Annie had no idea what was ahead. Maybe nothing. She might just go on getting nowhere making no real impression on him. She was a natural charmer, but fluttering long lashes at Adam would be a waste of time. That way she would only make a fool of herself. Well, she would turn in a good story, she would show him she was a good reporter, at least she could earn his professional approval.

She lay tossing for a long time, wondering what to do, and when she tried to stop thinking—because this way she would never get to sleep—she imagined his arms holding her. She could see his face, feel his breath on her eyes, his mouth on her mouth, and it was so real that she turned her head, and muffled her moans in a pillow.

She must have fallen asleep at last, because she woke before the alarm rang and her mother called her, but her dreams had been disturbing and she felt like a wet rag. Nobody had ever blown her peace of mind before like Adam Corbett. She was infatuated with him. This was the schoolgirl crush she had never had. A yearning for the unobtainable had been a way of life for most of her friends. They had worshipped pop stars and TV characters, men who were out of reach, even while they were settling for the boy they could get. But Annie had never daydreamed of a fantasy lover, much less had her sleep haunted with wild erotic dreams.

She jerked into her aerobics, forcing a faster pace than usual, and spending longer than usual on her make-up. She wasn't using much make-up during this heatwave, her skin was warm honey this summer, everybody looked healthier. But she smudged on bronze shadow that brought out the gold glints in her hazel eyes, and carefully painted her lips a shiny coral, although the first cup of hot coffee would see that off.

She wanted to look her best. She had never lacked confidence, but now she stared glumly at her reflection in her dressing table mirror. I look like a walking, talking doll, she thought. I might pass for sexy round here, but not where Adam has been. Her expression was wistful, her eyes were yearning, and she must watch this. She mustn't let anyone catch her mooning over Adam. If it was suspected at the office that Annie was getting a crush it would be the joke of the year. And if her parents had a clue how she felt God knows how they would react. Adam would be able to deal with it, but she would never dare look him in the face again.

What I want, she repeated in her mind and to her reflection, is for him to like me, to talk to me, to admit I'm good at my job. I fancy him incredibly, but that doesn't enter into it at this stage. Today what I have to do is go to work and keep my head, and nobody will know that anything has happened to me.

Come to that, nothing had. Except that her bones liquefied whenever she thought of him and if she let herself go on thinking an ache spread from the pit of her stomach to temples and fingertips, so that she felt like someone going down with a very vicious virus.

She was late, as usual, getting down to breakfast, drinking her coffee as she scooped up her bag. Her mother said nothing about last night. This morning, in the few minutes while Annie was rushing around, she said that she hoped that when Annie phoned the garage they would tell her that the car was scrap, because it wasn't safe on the roads, her mother was sure of that. 'I'll leave it to them,' said Annie, 'but if they can patch her up I'd like her back.'

'Your mother's right about the car,' said her father, driving her to work.

'I know,' said Annie. 'Dad, about Adam, does he have any family? Anyone else around here?'

'There was just his father.' Douglas Bennett concentrated on the road.

'What about him?'

'He was in the army—same regiment. We were together in the war. He was a regular—nice chap. Adam was away at school most of the time after his mother died, that was early on. John Corbett died the year after Adam started on the *Bugle*.'

He looked sidewards at his daughter, 'Anything else you'd like to know?' and she smiled back,

'I'm curious, that's all. He's the new editor, I'd like to know a bit about his background.'

'Nice chap,' said her father again and she said,

'Adam? I shouldn't think so,' and before her father could ask what that meant, she made him chuckle with an account of yesterday's interview with Jud Dane.

As soon as she got into the office she rang the garage. During the last twelve months her car had been regularly in and out of there. The bills were getting larger and the diagnoses more ominous, and when the mechanic came on the line she asked, 'Is it a write-off this time?'

'Well, I'll tell you. What you've got this time is the starter motor. We can fix that, but, he paused ominously and she held her breath, 'the brakes are dodgy.'

She hadn't noticed any trouble with braking. 'How much, the starter motor?' she asked.

'An exchange, twenty-five to thirty.' She couldn't afford it, but she wanted her car back on the road. 'O.K.,' she decided. 'Do the starter, and I'll bring it in again for the brakes.'

'You'll find it cheaper in the long run to get another,' Megan said sagely as Annie put down the phone.

'I know,' said Annie. 'But it's like an old hound-dog, I just can't bear to have it put down. You'll never guess who my father brought home to supper last night.'

'Astonish me,' said Megan, and Annie told her, adding that it had been a pleasant evening. 'When he's off duty,' she said, 'he's very good company.'

'That doesn't surprise me,' said Megan. 'When he's on duty you could hardly call him dull.'

'Well—no,' Annie agreed.

The heatwave showed no sign of breaking, and if Rocky had still been editor an easygoing mood would have been on them all. But Adam Corbett's presence was already causing a change of pace. Annie seemed to be the only member of the staff whose work had been handed back, but there was a general sharpening up. He was at the top of his profession; there was never any doubt who was in charge, but he put on no side.

What would have astonished Megan would have been if Annie had told her that she had stumbled accidentally against Adam in the garden last night, and that brief contact had stirred her more than if any other man had been kissing her with deep expertise. She had fallen for the first time in her life, and it was a situation she didn't know how to handle.

This morning she had the Jud Dane story to deal with. 'Good job he comes home again to Wales sometimes,' she said. There was a beauty queen from Carmarthen, photographed with Jud Dane on an earlier visit. His first wife, who had married him at eighteen, had been the girl next door, and Annie went along to the drinks machine, got herself a plastic cup of coffee, and settled down with one of the phones in the reporters' room.

First she rang a Swansea journalist she knew and asked him if the first Mrs 'Dane' was still living around there, and was off to a flying start. Mrs Griffith, as she had been, and Mrs Thomas as she was now, worked in a local baker's shop. Annie thanked her informant and wrote down the address, and within the next half hour had the phone number of the beauty queen.

It was possible, of course, that they were all going to say only flattering things about Jud, in which case his own good opinion of himself would be justified. Annie got the beauty queen on the phone, introduced herself and explained, 'I'm writing an article on Jud Dane, the rock singer, I believe you and he are friends?'

'You got me out of the bath to talk about him?' said the beauty queen. 'Well, what do you want to know?'

'He says he's a very lonely man these days,' said Annie.

'Oh, I had that one,' said Ceridwen, 'and "I can help you get into show business, little girl. There's this TV show".'

Annie began to laugh, 'He was on the way to saying that to me. He said he got you an audition with Harlech TV . . .' 'She was terrible,' he had said.

'Audition?' shrieked Ceridwen. 'Never! I never got anywhere near a TV camera. He's a slob. Off stage he's a dead loss, and you know what I mean if he's telling you the tale.'

'Could I come along and see you?' asked Annie. The picture was of Ceridwen, being crowned as carnival queen by Jud and looking up adoringly at him. A new photograph alongside that might make a nice contrast.

'How's it going?' asked Megan when it was almost lunchtime. By then Annie had made several more phone calls, written several more pages of notes, and was on her third cup of coffee.

'He loves 'em and leaves 'em,' said Annie. 'So far as women go he's a creep. They're telling me things we can't print in a family paper.'

'Sounds promising,' said Megan. 'Coming out to lunch?'

'Give me five minutes.'

Annie gathered up her notes and went along to the editor's room and knocked on the door. From inside Adam called, 'Come in.' He was on the phone, listening, saying, 'Yes,' and not much more, but she was sure it was someone he knew well and liked, and when he said, 'Right then, I'll see you,' and put down the phone the words, 'Who was that?' rose to her lips.

She managed to hold them back, which was a narrow escape because it was none of her business and he would have told her so, he was the last man alive to take liberties with. She said, 'I've been on the Jud Dane interview all morning, and got some super stuff. Would you like to see the notes?'

'I'd like to see the finished interview,' he said.

Annie wished he had held out a hand for her notes, although nobody could read her shorthand but her. Then she could have started to translate for him and maybe said, 'Megan and I are just off to lunch, will you join us?' And Megan, who could be tactful at times, might have found she had to hang on for a phone call when Annie dashed along to the office and told her. But he didn't want to see the notes, and the question, 'Are you coming out to lunch?' stuck, so that she just stood there and after a few moments she said, 'He's looking for his ideal girl, but he's asking for more than he delivers. They all said he thought he was irresistible, but he certainly wasn't. And I can vouch for that.'

'You can?'

'He propositioned me, didn't he? He came swaggering down from that stage——' It *was* funny, it had made Megan laugh, and Adam was smiling, but she was almost sure he thought she was showing off.

'You're not surprised?' she queried.

'Were you?'

'No.' Yes, would have been mock modesty. 'But I was warned by one of the girls that the great lover is a dead loss off stage, if I knew what she meant,' and this time she *did* make Adam laugh.

'You're incorrigible,' he said, and he picked up the phone again so that she had to get out.

It had always been easy before. After she had nearly fallen into the marriage trap with David she had never had any difficulty controlling her emotions, so that it didn't hurt too much when the men in her life started to act like Huw. But with Adam she was confused, trying to keep her distance but longing to be near him. Of course he was different. He had been to more places and done more things than any other man she had ever met. He was stimulating and exciting, and as Megan said, 'dead sexy', and Annie was falling for him. Or would be if she didn't watch out . . .

The story kept her occupied all afternoon, and tomorrow she was off to see Ceridwen Owen and the first Mrs Dane, taking Charlie with her for photographs. She didn't see Adam again, and Megan and Tom gave her lift home when Tom collected Megan from work.

Her mother was turning out the studio. She hadn't used it much this summer, but she was out there when Annie arrived home. The evening meal was a salad and cold meats, and Catlin, said Annie's father, had been spring-cleaning since midday.

The studio was a big airy room. Light streamed down from a large window in the roof. There were bright red Turkish rugs on the floor and the furniture was a huge old desk, a couple of chairs and a studio couch. Catrin was up a ladder, giving a fresh coat of white paint to her third wall, when Annie climbed the iron staircase to the old loft and demanded, 'What *do* you think you're doing?'

'Hush,' hissed her mother. 'Your father thinks I'm just cleaning. I don't want him to know. He ought not to be balancing up stepladders.'

'Neither should you,' said Annie. 'Come on, I'll finish it. Why didn't you say you wanted it doing?'

She reached up to help her mother down, and Catrin asked, 'Aren't you going out anywhere tonight?'

'No.'

'Anybody coming here?'

'Not that I know of.'

'Not Adam? I thought—well, you've been together all day, I thought you might have fixed up something for this evening.'

'We have not been together all day,' Annie pointed out, 'I've hardly seen him—he's the editor. I don't suppose he'll ask me to marry him before the end of the week.'

Her mother looked martyred, and Annie said crossly, 'Well, it's ridiculous, and I've told you to forget it, Adam is never going to be interested in me. And it doesn't bother me at all, I wouldn't want it any other way.'

She hoped that was emphatic enough without sounding emotional, because she would not have had her mother guess for the world that, short of murder, she couldn't think of much she would not risk if she considered it likely to capture and hold Adam Corbett's attention.

'How about you and me having a meal some evening?' Charlie asked her as they set off to interview Ceridwen Owen and the first Mrs Jud Dane. They were using Charlie's car, which he drove recklessly, but if Annie had said, 'Slow down,' that would have made him show off even more, because he thought he was a wonderful driver.

Every time Annie was between boy-friends Charlie made a pass, but Annie never took him up. Spending most of today with him was bad enough, he would be talking about himself most of the time and she certainly wasn't meeting him after work.

She said yes, she and Huw had come to the parting, but she wasn't dating anybody right now. 'You don't know what you're missing,' said Charlie, and she laughed.

'That's more or less what Jud Dane told me, and you should read what some of his exes say about him!'

Ceridwen, the beauty queen, was a tall busty blonde, working as a receptionist in a Caernarvon hotel. She was waiting for them in the foyer, and she took them over the road to the apartment she shared with two other girls on the hotel staff.

There Charlie took a photograph of Ceridwen smiling radiantly. He promised to send her a copy of that, but it wasn't what the article needed, and when Annie said, 'I wanted to talk to you about Jud Dane,' Ceridwen's expression changed as though she had bitten into a lemon.

It took them all day. They stopped for a sandwich

lunch at a roadside pub and caught Mrs Dane number one during the afternoon, behind the counter at the cake shop, just as Annie had been told.

'Are you Mrs Thomas?' she asked the younger of the two women, and the older said,

'That's me.' She had greying hair and she was matronly plump, and it was easy to see that Jud Dane had left her behind a long time ago.

Annie introduced herself and Charlie, and said that they were doing an article on Jud Dane, who used to be Dai Griffith.

'Reporters, is it?' She smiled at them. 'I can't be telling you anything about Dai, I haven't seen him for over twenty years. Done well for himself—but you know that, don't you? I was eighteen when I married him, he was coming up to twenty-four. It only lasted six months and then he was away.' It was as if she was talking about a girl who was a stranger to her.

She had had no letters, no contact, no money. When his first record reached the charts Dai had changed his name and deserted his soft-spoken little Welsh wife. Annie wondered if she had loved him although she looked content enough now. 'Married two more, didn't he?' said Mrs Thomas. 'He was always one for the girls, mind you.'

'He says he's still looking for true love,' said Annie, and Mrs Thomas rocked with laughter.

'He found true love years ago, did Dai. Every time he looked in a mirror!'

'What are you doing tonight?' Charlie asked as they approached the outskirts of their home town.

What I would like to do, Annie thought, is go and find Adam. She had never sought out a man before, they had always come looking for her. But if she didn't see Adam tonight she didn't think she could go home and expect to sleep when she went to bed. She might dream about him again, but she wanted to see him, and for the first time she understood how infatuation made folk hang around outside houses or walk up and down streets just to catch a glimpse of the one they were hooked on. It was like a drug. Just a few words would be a fix that should see her through the night. She put her hands over her eyes briefly and said, 'I could use a drink.'

'So could I,' said Charlie.

Going in with Charlie would look less obvious than strolling into the hotel alone. 'Let's go to the Bodlyn,' she said. 'Jud Dane's lot are holed up at the Grand, and I don't want to bump into them.'

Adam was staying at the Bodlyn Arms, although he might not be downstairs in the public rooms. If I don't see him, she decided, I shall ask for him, and if he's in the hotel I shall ring his room and say, 'Do come down, Charlie and I would like to tell you how our day went.'

A windowed wall separated the lounge bar from the restaurant and she saw Adam right away, sitting in the far corner of the dining room. There was a woman at his table, and while Charlie went to the bar to get drinks Annie sat down, snuggling low into her chair so that she was out of sight.

She had wanted to run to him. She felt as if she had strayed into a magnetic field and was literally being pulled. She gripped the arm of her chair, and when Charlie brought her a vodka and tonic she took a good gulp and said, 'How about eating here?'

'All right.' Charlie's eyes gleamed, and Annie hoped he wasn't wondering if this affability on her part might develop into spending a night together.

There were plenty of empty tables. As they walked through the door the dining room was deserted up this end, and Annie said brightly, 'Why, there's Adam over there! Shall we join them?'

Charlie was aghast, 'We can't muscle in on him, for

God's sake!' He grabbed her elbow, hissing through the side of his mouth, 'It's because you don't cut any ice with him, isn't it? Because he didn't give you a second look yesterday morning. Got a little bet with yourself, have you, that you'll get him? You can have a bet with me if you like. Not a chance!'

She knew she was crazy trying to break in between Adam and his companion. But Charlie couldn't have held her back, even if his grip had tightened instead of loosening, and she threaded her way between the tables towards that table in the far corner.

CHAPTER FOUR

THE girl with Adam was talking earnestly as Annie walked towards them, gesturing so that rings flashed white fire on her fingers. She had thick dark hair, cut straight in a fringe and bob, and a gold slave bangle worn high on a smooth sun-tanned arm.

They were deep in discussion, speaking the same language, Annie knew, although Adam sat back in his chair and the girl leaned forward. There were coffee cups on the table and a cheeseboard, and a lemon sorbet in a little silver dish on the girl's plate.

Annie saw everything in sharp detail, like a spotlit scene on a darkened stage. Adam and this girl. She could imagine their talk, Adam's deep voice and the girl's husky tones. The room seemed very long and she seemed to make slow dreamlike progress. Adam looked down the room and saw her, then said something to the girl, who turned her head.

She had high cheekbones that went well with her hairstyle. She was very striking, and Annie wished she had the strength and the sense to smile a greeting and then sit down some distance away with her back to them. Then they might believe that her being here was a coincidence, but she kept going.

'Hello,' said Adam when she reached them. Charlie was grinning sheepishly and the girl smiled at Charlie, ignoring Annie. 'This is Anna Bennett, one of our reporters,' said Adam, 'and Charles Mann.' Charlie's role was obvious from the camera equipment slung around him, and the girl said,

'Ah, the staff of the *Bugle*.'

'There are a few more of us,' said Annie, and then the girl looked at her.

'I'm Eunice Fleming,' she said.

The one who wrote clever books about women leading gloomy lives. Annie had never read one through to the end, and it was no use pretending she had, because Eunice Fleming was summing her up with hard bright eyes.

Charlie pulled out a chair at another table and Annie sat down, and Adam asked, 'How did the interviews go?'

'Not badly at all,' said Annie. 'Quite well, actually.'

Of course they were not being invited to join Adam and Eunice, whose meal was nearly finished and who obviously needed nobody else. A waiter presented menus and Annie scanned hers and asked what Charlie was having, and hoped she would be able to swallow, because her throat was aching as if she was holding back tears.

She managed to keep up a cheerful repartee to Charlie's flirtatious banter, but all the time she was conscious of Adam. She couldn't see him, she couldn't really hear him, but although she kept looking at Charlie and the menu all her senses seemed tuned to Adam.

She decided on avocado with vinaigrette dressing and sole Mornay, and Charlie chose green pea soup and sirloin steak, then she remembered that her parents would be waiting for their evening meal until she got home, and her hands were grubby pointing out her selection on the menu.

While the waiter scribbled down the order she said, 'I won't be a minute, I'd like to wash my hands.'

Eunice came into the Ladies as Annie rinsed her hands under the tap. There was no one else in the room and Eunice paused for a moment in front of a mirror to smooth down her hair, although Annie couldn't see a hair out of place.

Then Eunice said, 'A disappointment, was it!' She didn't have a husky voice, she had a crisp snappy voice. She was much taller than Annie and when she looked at Annie she looked down her nose. 'Did you think Adam would be alone?'

Annie hadn't stopped to think, but that was what she had hoped. She pressed the heater button and turned her hands in the waves of warm air and said, 'I didn't think about it at all.'

'Then you should.' Eunice was very brisk, very businesslike. 'It must be exciting for you to be working with a journalist of his calibre, and up to a point fan-worship is flattering. I speak from experience, of course, I have a great many fans myself, and I can understand you being dazzled by Adam. You wouldn't be the first, believe me, but you mustn't pester him after office hours. No doubt you'd love to be his pupil, but I don't think he'll be giving you any homework.'

Eunice was not talking about journalism, Annie knew, and her temper flared, making her say silkily, 'But I'm sure he's a marvellous teacher and I'm sure there's such a lot I could learn from him.'

That was stupid. Eunice Fleming was maddening, but there was no sense in provoking her. Although she didn't seem provoked, only even more supercilious, smiling and sneering, 'Oh, you're pretty enough, but it takes rather more than a pretty face to interest Adam.' She meant that Annie was dim, compared with Adam, compared with herself. 'In fact when he saw you coming just now he said——' The hot air drier stopped and everything seemed quiet as Eunice stopped speaking. Then she shrugged, 'Oh, forget it.'

She was not sparing Annie's feelings. She knew that leaving it like that would make Annie imagine all sorts of things, and Annie had to bite her tongue to stop herself blurting out, 'What *did* he say?' Instead she said, 'Excuse me, I have to make a phone call.'

She had to wait a few minutes to get into the phone booth to tell her father that she was having a meal in town but she wouldn't be late.

'Who with?' he asked.

'Charlie Mann. I've ordered, I must dash.'

She wished she didn't have to go back into the dining room. What had Adam said about her? It was only a word, because she had seen him speak. It couldn't have been much. It could hardly have been anything, but Annie must have walked down that long room with her eyes fixed on Adam, and Eunice had noted that. She sounded used to it—'You wouldn't be the first, believe me'—and it didn't worry her. Eunice Fleming was very sure of herself, and Charlie had told Annie she was behaving like an idiot. But Charlie thought it was the challenge that Adam Corbett represented, and Charlie must never guess that she had a crush on the man. She had to go back now and take the drama out of this, or heaven knows what Charlie would be telling them all in the office in the morning.

'I rang home,' she explained. The starters had been served and Charlie was halfway through his soup. Several more diners had arrived. There was enough noise now to drown the conversation from this table, so that Adam and Eunice couldn't overhear what was being said by Annie and Charlie even if they'd tried. Which they didn't, of course. When Annie glanced casually across she saw that neither of them was looking her way.

She put on a show of good spirits, and when Adam and Eunice passed and said goodnight she beamed at them both. As they left the dining room, two tall handsome distinguished people whom most of the diners had turned to watch, she clapped a hand across her mouth as though stifling laughter. 'How about that?' she gurgled. 'She followed me to the washroom!' Charlie must not know that in her mind's eye Annie was following them upstairs. And then . . . she wouldn't think what might happen then . . .

'Yeah?' said Charlie.

'Guess why? To say she understands all about fans herself, having so many, and she knows what a thrill it must be for us having somebody as famous as Adam running our piffling little paper, but please don't badger him after office hours.'

'Why has she got fans?' Charlie enquired. 'Is she an actress or something?'

'Something,' said Annie. 'She writes sexy books.'

'Yeah?' said Charlie again. 'I must get one out of the library,' and Annie grinned.

'I shouldn't bother. They talk all the time.'

They ate their meal and she paid her half of the bill, and as Charlie opened the door of his car in the parking lot he said, 'My place?'

'Sorry.'

'No afters?'

'That apple pie was your afters, but I'd appreciate a lift home.'

He gave in. Charlie was never short of a pretty girl, and Annie was a shade too bright for his tastes. He was not entirely at ease with the clever ones. All the same, if she thought Adam Corbett might fall for her she wasn't so smart, and driving along he asked, 'Did you really go looking for him tonight?'

'Not till I saw him when we walked into the dining room. Then I thought it might be a laugh to march up and get introduced to his girl-friend.'

'Do you fancy him?'

She answered without a tremor, 'Of course, we all do,' and laughed. 'But he's too old for me.'

'He's only around my age,' Charlie protested. She supposed he was, but he had none of Charlie's small-boy mannerisms. Adam was a man, with a world of experience and sexual magnetism.

'Like I said,' she joked, 'he's getting on.'

'I wonder if she's staying here,' mused Charlie. 'He writes books as well, doesn't he? Perhaps she'll move in with him and they'll share a room and a desk.' He chuckled. 'And the rest. They looked to me as if they were used to getting together.'

'Sounds cosy,' said Annie, and felt the cold of winter settle on her although the night was warm.

When she got out of Charlie's car at her gate lights were on, so her parents were still up. As Charlie drove away she looked up and down the quiet road and it seemed full of shadows.

Her parents knew Charlie, but they weren't interested in him. Her mother asked what she'd had to eat and Annie told them, then yawned and said she was tired, it had been a long day and she thought she'd go up to bed.

She soaked in a hot bath first. It was more than likely that Eunice Fleming was staying at Adam's hotel, in a room conveniently near to his, and lying in the warm scented water Annie imagined Eunice, naked and perfumed, in a bath, in a bed, waiting for Adam. And Adam coming to her—and she knew she was being so stupid, lying here punishing herself.

This was how it felt to be jealous, and she was sorry now for Huw, and for anyone else who had felt like this about her, because it really did hurt badly.

She got into bed and read a thriller until her eyes blurred, but even then as soon as she switched off the light and let her eyelids close she found herself sighing again. Getting over this infatuation that had struck her like a sudden fever was going to be a struggle, but she would have to be her own doctor and heal herself.

'Did you see Adam yesterday?' her mother asked her at breakfast.

'Of course,' said Annie, 'I work with him.' She hadn't told them they had eaten at adjoining tables, nor about Eunice.

'Do you think he's comfortable at that hotel?' asked her mother, and that was unconsciously ironic and Annie replied drily,

'All the comforts of home, I should think.'

Annie was down for the magistrates' courts at ten o'clock, but until then she worked on the Jud Dane story, and with yesterday's interviews fresh in her mind her fingers flew over the keys.

During the afternoon Charlie brought down the photographs. There was a gem of a picture of Ceridwen which told a vivid story. You could almost hear the disdainful sniff with which she had greeted the name of Jud Dane. The study of 'Dai's' wife was good too. Sian Thomas looked what she was, a contented sensible hardworking woman. When she said Dai's only true love was himself it wasn't bitterness, but it was the truth.

'Smashing,' said Annie, gathering them up with the pages she had written. 'Let's show Adam.'

Adam was typing on a big office typewriter, but he sat back and looked at Charlie's photographs and said they were excellent, and Charlie grinned and squirmed with delight.

He read Annie's copy and said, 'Very good,' and Charlie chortled, 'We make a good team.'

'You do mean working,' Annie stressed, and Charlie went on grinning. As they turned to go Adam said, 'Annie, a moment,' and she hung back until Charlie had closed the door. Then Adam said, 'Is it just a working partnership?'

'Of course.' The only reason he was asking was that they were both on his staff, because he said,

'Well, don't play him up so that we have trouble with Charlie. You seem to have a talent for making waves. What did you say to Eunice?'

She could swear he was amused even if he wasn't

smiling, and she wasn't sorry to hear that she had succeeded in rattling Eunice. 'I cheeked her back,' she said. 'She's a very superior lady.'

'No doubt you gave as good as you got. The story's working out, we'll make a journalist of you yet.'

'Thank you, sir, that would be much appreciated, and may I say, sir, that you're being a big inspiration to all us small town hacks.' She left him laughing, but he wouldn't have laughed if she had asked the question that was burning in her brain—'Did you sleep with Eunice last night?'

Thanks to Charlie it was all round the office today that Miss Fleming had been tête-a-tête with Adam Corbett in the Bodlyn Arms last night, and Megan had wondered if they might get an interview with her for the women's page. After all, she was a famous novelist, what did Annie think, as Annie had met and talked to her?

'I wouldn't say I talked *to* her,' said Annie. 'She looked down her nose and talked *at* me. Why don't you ask Adam?'

She couldn't face asking Eunice personal questions. If Eunice agreed she hoped that Megan would do the interview herself, and Megan came back to say that next time Eunice Fleming came to Llanaven Adam was sure she could spare the *Bugle* an hour or two of her time.

'She's gone, then?' asked Annie, very casually.

'Left this morning,' said Megan. 'I'd have stayed on a bit longer if it had been me, wouldn't you?'

'Have a heart,' said Annie gaily, 'he is convalescent,' and pain twisted inside her, stiffening her fingers on the keys of the typewriter.

The first *Llanaven Bugle* produced under Adam Corbett's editorship was probably the best in its seventy-odd years of publication. It was still a small town paper, full of small town news, but the copy was crisper, better written. The features still had the same bylines, but they had fresh angles, they were thought provoking. The new man in charge had advised 'Try this,' or 'Follow that up,' and the article on Jud Dane by Anna Bennett was the liveliest she had ever written.

There was a picture of Jud in one of his favourite poses, legs astride, arms folded, looking handsome and arrogant, with his description of himself . . . tender . . . passionate . . . generous; and what he was looking for in a woman. Then the ex-wives and girl-friends, responding to what he had said about them with a few pithy comments, and Charlie's photograph of Ceridwen Owen summing up the general opinion.

There were going to be furious letters from his fans to the editor, although no one was suggesting he was not a talented singer; but the article would make most of the readers chuckle.

The first reader reaction was waiting when Annie arrived on Friday morning, in the shape of a large and angry man. When she walked into her office he jumped up, and Megan, who had asked if she could help and been told no, jumped up too.

It was Annie he was here to see, and he proceeded to wave the *Bugle* under her nose. He was Jud Dane's public relations man, and this was not the kind of publicity they wanted. He would get her blacklisted, he roared, nobody else in show business would ever give her another interview. She would be hearing from the lawyers within hours because this was defamation of character, and by the time they were through with her and her pathetic little rag she would wish she had never heard the name of Jud Dane.

He was bellowing like a bull, so red-faced and red-eyed that he was surely risking a seizure. John Hogan came hurrying in, but there was no chance of him being heard. Annie could see his lips moving, but it was her the P.R.O. was raging at, still flailing the air with his newspaper as though he expected her to cower and she would be damned if she would.

By now the room was filling. The noise had brought in most of the editorial staff; there weren't many shouting matches at the *Bugle*. Rocky would have been apologising humbly, promising anything, but the article would never have seen the light of day while Rocky was editor.

When Adam appeared in the doorway the din was deafening. All the men seemed to be shouting, although no one was actually laying hands on this beefy belligerent character. When Adam looked into the room his staff shut up, the man in charge was here, so that the P.R.O. was the only one still shouting, and in the sudden silence he stopped for breath.

He saw Adam at the same time. 'You're the editor?' he demanded.

'Yes.'

'Well, boyo, you're in trouble! You're finished! This little hatchet job is going to cost you yours!'

He had stormed in here to wipe the floor with all of them, but this man stood a head taller than any and there was no expression at all on his face. Only his eyes moved, and they were steely. When he spoke he sounded bored. 'If we'd been doing a hatchet job,' he drawled, 'we'd have started in Amsterdam.'

'What?'

'Last November, wasn't it? I can give you five minutes.' Adam turned and the beefy man went after him, and so did Annie. While the others started asking each other what Adam had meant she intended finding out, and she kept on the heels of the P.R. man.

Adam sat down at his desk. The P.R.O. halted just in front of it and Annie stood back a little, watching and listening. This was fascinating. Without saying a word Adam dominated. The man seemed to shrink in front of her eyes, the furious flush in his face fading into bluish blotches, although he was still trying to bluster, 'What's all this about Amsterdam?'

'Just reminding you what a real exposé could turn up,' said Adam. 'This article is nothing. Your client should count himself lucky.'

'Is this a personal thing?'

'I've never met the man and I've no particular interest in him, but I get around.'

'And you're the editor of the *Llanaven Bugle*?' He went on staring. 'Don't I know you? Who are you?'

'Corbett—Adam Corbett.'

The man was still fogged. 'What are you doing here?'

'Taking a break,' said Adam.

'Of course.' He remembered then. Corbett was still walking with a stick, although he hardly seemed to need it, and there was no way anyone was going to pressure him into climbing down. If he got his knife into Jud there'd be some squealing down. The man's tone changed completely. 'It's made him look a fool.'

'He is a fool,' said Adam.

'That isn't going to help me,' the man said ruefully. 'He was carrying on like a bloody maniac this morning after he saw what she'd written. It's you he's got it in for, my girl.' Annie shrugged. She could manage to live with Jud Dane's displeasure, and it had been splendid the way Adam had handled this, she couldn't remember when she had enjoyed anything more. 'He thought he'd got you where he wanted you. He thought you'd be bringing a nice little story round to show him tonight.' She couldn't help a small grimace at that. 'I should keep out of dark alleys if I were you,' he added. 'He might be sending some of the boys looking for you.'

He gave a half grin when he said that. He wanted her to be frightened, but he didn't want Corbett antagonised, so he tried to make it seem like a friendly warning, nothing to do with him but something to bear in mind.

The smirk set when he looked back at Adam, who

was almost smiling and who said almost gently, 'Tell the boys, boyo, that I've walked down more dark alleys than they've had hot dinners. If they're looking for trouble I can teach them a few tricks in street fighting. And remind your boss I don't play by the rules in my trade either.'

The P.R.O. was not tangling here. He knew what a brilliant and ruthless journalist could do, muckraking around Jud Dane. 'I hope you're not doing any follow-ups,' he said darkly.

'Not unless he makes the idea tempting,' said Adam.

'Trust me,' said the P.R.O., who looked, Annie thought, thoroughly untrustworthy, although in this case she believed him. When he had gone she asked,

'What happened in Amsterdam?'

'Nothing for the *Bugle*.'

'Will you use it? Would it be a big story?'

'No, I shan't use it. Jud Dane's secrets are small fry.'

They wouldn't be small fry here because they were all small fry here, and she wondered how long it would be before Adam became bored with them. 'Well,' she said lightly, 'I'll keep out of dark alleys, like the man said.'

'Did he scare you?'

'Not at all,' she answered, smiling. At no stage had she felt frightened or even threatened. She was surrounded by colleagues and she did not scare easily. And from the moment Adam walked in the only frightened one had been the P.R. man. But no sooner had Annie spoken than she realised she had missed a chance of pretending it had all been dreadful. Then he might have reassured and comforted her. She was a small girl, and that had been a hulking great thug shouting at her, and then warning her that the heavy mob might be cornering her in a dark alley. It would have been understandable if she had been upset, but she didn't think Adam would be convinced if she changed her mind now and burst into tears.

She didn't think she could fool him, except in the way she was fooling them all, about how obsessed she was with him. No other man had ever brought her flying into the office each morning because here she would see him and speak to him, and made her feel empty and aching when he wasn't near.

A little of Adam Corbett's charisma was rubbing off on everyone on the *Bugle*. The staff were smartening up their ideas because he was such a cracking good journalist, and even Miss Grey, who had been Rocky's secretary for years and was Adam's now, who was well over fifty, was going around with a spring in her step and a henna rinse on her crimped coiffure.

The girl on the switchboard monitored the telephone calls that came for him and reported that he could have been eating out every night, he was getting the invitations but turning them down, explaining that he was working on his book in the evenings, in his hotel.

Annie never saw him out of the office. She had put out hints, keeping it light and bright and friendly. If he had been at all interested he could have followed something up, but he didn't. There was no lessening the distance he kept between himself and the rest, and Annie was one of the rest. Unlike Eunice, of course—and how she hated Eunice!

All day her article on Jud Dane was stirring things. The switchboard was kept busy, her colleagues couldn't stop talking about how Adam had dealt with the public relations man, and when she got home that evening her father said he had got a good laugh out of it.

Her mother said nothing until they were sitting down to their meal. Catrin preferred reading nice things about people. She thought this was too sharp by half, going out of its way to offend, and when Annie said it had been fun writing it Catrin sighed, 'I do hope you're not going to turn into one of those hardbitten career women.'

'Blame Adam Corbett,' said Annie. 'He's calling the tune for all of us.'

She only mentioned Adam's name when she couldn't help it. She knew that her mother was ready to pounce on any mention of him, and now Catrin asked, 'You are getting on all right with Adam, aren't you?'

'Of course.'

'He hasn't——' Catrin stirred the croutons in her soup, slowly, making a pattern with them, and Annie said sharply,

'Made a pass at me? No. And he isn't going to, so don't start that again.' There was a short silence, then Catrin asked,

'Any plans for the weekend?' and as if this would be better than nothing, 'Will you be seeing Huw?'

Huw had phoned here on Wednesday night, and Annie had kept the conversation brief and put down the phone gently but firmly, 'No, I won't,' she said. 'I haven't made up my mind what I'll be doing.'

There was always something happening over the weekend. There was the barbecue tomorrow that Robert Marsden had phoned her about, and when he rang again, later this evening, to see if she had changed her mind, she said, 'All right.' If her mother started to wonder why she was spending her evenings watching television, washing her hair, reading in her room, she might decide that Annie was missing Huw. If he phoned again and Annie didn't catch the call Catrin could be suggesting he came round and talked things over.

Besides, it might get Annie's mind off Adam. If she wasn't working, if she didn't *have* to focus on something else, thoughts of Adam filled her like a physical presence. While she was waiting for Robert to come and collect her she thought, if Adam was coming for me I should be off my head with excitement.

She was wearing a tangerine silk blouse, a full cotton caramel-coloured skirt and matching pumps. Usually she wore small stud earrings, tonight she had on a pair of heavy gipsy rings that swung when she tossed her head, and she stood at her bedroom window and imagined that a taxi would draw up, any minute now, and Adam would get out. She wondered what kind of car he would drive as soon as that leg mended. She desperately wished him here.

All her life most of her wishes had come true, and this intense and hopeless longing was new to her. When the car did draw up she saw Adam for a moment in the driver's seat. It was Robert who got out, the only man in the car, and she knew that, but she still saw Adam.

She went downstairs and her father called from behind his newspaper in the lounge, 'Have a nice time.'

'I always do,' she called back, picking up two bottles of white wine from the hall table. Her mother came out of the lounge to go to the front door with her as the bell rang.

'I didn't think you liked Robert,' said Catrin.

'He's only giving me a lift there,' said Annie. 'I'll know most of the others.' Catrin looked thoughtful. Annie had caught that expression several times this week and wondered if her mother was up to anything.

When she opened the door Robert almost smacked his lips and informed her that she looked, 'Very tasty.' And she thought that her father was right, he did have a foxy face, and she said, 'Thank you, but I think I should warn you, I'm a tough bird.'

The barbecue was in aid of the local rugby club's pavilion, which had developed wet rot. It was held in one of the biggest gardens in town, the weather was still perfect and there was a good attendance. Annie would not have been surprised to see Huw, it wouldn't have bothered her; but he wasn't there, although most of the faces were familiar.

She was popular, she was pretty, she was fun. She was at the centre of things all evening, and her article on Jud Dane came in for discussion. Some of the girls said they didn't believe a word of it. Music played from loudspeakers and they danced on the lawns between the trees. Barbecued steaks and sausages sizzled and spluttered over charcoal grids, and everybody had brought a bottle, and Annie danced, with Robert and with others.

Everyone knew by now that she and Huw had split up, and Robert was trying to stress that he was her new man and fooling nobody. She had more than a few offers as the night wore on, and she talked and laughed and flirted and looked as if she was having a wonderful time. She lost count of the glasses she was emptying. Nobody was counting. It was only wine, but it was way beyond her usual consumption and it wasn't even helping.

She was *not* having a wonderful time. These were folk she had known for years, most of them were her friends, she liked most of them, but she felt as though not one of them was real. It was nightmarish. She was alone, moving among shadows, and suppose it was always going to be like this, with Adam Corbett obsessing her so completely that without him even in the thickest crowd she would always be alone.

She was having a miserable time. She wished she hadn't come and she wondered how soon she could leave. The barbecue was ending with bacon and eggs at dawn, but when a couple who lived her way said cheerio just after midnight she asked if they would give her a lift. Sure, they said, and Annie slipped away with them, climbing unsteadily into the back of their car.

'I hope you've drunk less than I have,' she said.

'He hasn't,' said his wife, 'but I have.' She was driving and she dropped Annie outside her home. Annie thanked them, and they all agreed it had been a really good evening, and she held on to the gate as the car drove away.

All the house windows were dark, and that was as well, because her mother would be shocked to see her woozy. But there was a glow from the loft, through the roof window. Her mother must have forgotten to turn off the light, she must have been up there this evening, it wasn't worth bothering about tonight.

But Annie found herself walking round the side of the house drawn by the niggling worry in her mind. When her father had had that heart attack he had lain senseless on the bedroom floor. Only for minutes, thank God, or it might have been a different story. Annie would have to go up there and make quite sure that this was a left-on light.

She called, 'Mother!' as she climbed the steps, and again as she opened the door. Then she stopped, her jaw fell open and her eyes went wide as saucers. She hardly recognised the room. She didn't know half the furniture in here. There were extra chairs, another small table. The divan was made up into a bed and the big desk was cleared of her mother's painting clutter. There was a typewriter on the desk and Adam was sitting behind it.

It *was* Adam, in the flesh, although Annie blinked several times to make sure. Then she demanded, 'What are you doing here?' Living here, by the looks of it. 'How long have you been here?'

'I moved in this evening.'

In the morning she would hear all about it. She knew what her parents' idea was, practically taking in Adam as a lodger, and that was fine by Annie. They expected her to object, but she couldn't be happier, she thought it would be lovely. 'Come in,' he said. 'I'll get you a black coffee.'

She sat down on one of the chairs she hadn't seen before, a club armchair in brown hide. Second-hand, obviously, but smelling of furniture polish. Her mother must have been round the junk shops or the auctions.

She had made this room into a very comfortable bedsitter. Annie sniffed the chair arm and said, 'Lavender—she must have been working like a beaver.'

Her voice seemed to be echoing. Her head was reeling now, the room was going gently up and down. She watched Adam and thought how splendid it was to find him here. He was wearing a dark blue dressing gown that looked thin and silky, dark trousers. He was very tall, but he moved quietly, and for some reason it reminded her of the crystal cave all those years ago, when she had squirmed through the crack in the rocks and thought she might find magic, shining and wonderful. She laughed about that as Adam handed her a mug of coffee.

It was hot. She had to be very careful. She took a few sips and then put down the mug, very slowly, beside her chair.

Adam was sitting at the desk again, elbow on the desk, chin on his hand, steady as a rock although the room was still going round. 'Do you do this often?' he asked.

'Do what?'

'Get drunk.'

Annie never got drunk. Tonight she had been trying to stop thinking about him, and it was his fault she was lightheaded. She wouldn't have had so many glasses of wine if she hadn't been so miserable. 'Tonight I had things on my mind,' she said sombrely.

'I see.'

He knew it all. She supposed that was part of his attraction, knowing so much. Being so clever as well as so sexy. But he didn't know this. 'Ah, but you don't,' she said. 'You don't have a clue what was on my mind. So I shall tell you.' Telling him seemed such a simple solution that she wondered why she hadn't done it before. 'You were,' she said, with a small smile of triumph because she had succeeded in surprising him.

At least he raised an eyebrow, and she went on, 'I have a terrible crush on you. Well, it's more than a crush—a fixation, I suppose, because I can't stop thinking about you. It's never happened to me before—nobody's ever made this kind of impression on me. I feel like a stick of Blackpool rock stamped all through with your name.'

That made her giggle. She got up, with the help of the chair's arm, and walked a few steps away, but her legs were rubbery and she sat down again on the edge of the divan that was made up as a bed. 'Please will you make love to me?' she said.

CHAPTER FIVE

'DRINK your coffee,' said Adam.

The coffee was over there, and anyhow, she didn't want it. She swung her feet up. The divan made a double bed, but Adam was so tall he would probably have to sleep diagonally, and he wasn't coming over. She didn't have to look to know, and she went on staring up at the black sky through the window in the roof like a hole in space.

'You don't think much of me, do you?' she said. 'You don't think about me at all. Do you suppose that's why I can't stop thinking about you?'

'More than likely.'

One of her earrings caught on the bedding and she jerked her head to free it. 'I suppose,' she said sadly, 'you've had so many women that your standards are terribly high. With all your experience you just don't fancy me.'

'I've had enough experience not to take advantage of girls who turn up stoned in the small hours,' he said.

That shook her. 'I am not stoned!' She tried to sit up, but the effort was too much and she let her head fall back again on the pillow, although she went on protesting, 'It was only wine, and I suppose I should have eaten something. They gave me a great thick steak, black and bloody at the same time. I fed it to one of the dogs.'

When Adam touched her she smiled up at him, but he was holding the coffee and she said, 'I don't want that.'

'You want it. Sit up.'

Somehow she did, and she got down most of the

cofee while he stood over her. Then she asked, 'If I don't say another word may I stay here?'

'No, you may not.'

'Well, I think you're being very mean, and I don't know how you imagine I'm going to climb down those steps unless you carry me.'

She got up then, and she should have been a mug of black coffee more sober by now, only it didn't seem to be working that way.

'If I do we might both break our necks,' he said. As he stooped to take the mug from her she saw the healing network of scars across his chest as the dressing gown fell open. He must have been terribly injured, lying there on the mountainside, and tears welled in her eyes for his pain. And for her own because she was being rejected. Although she wasn't too clear in her mind right now she knew that the crystal cave had gone dark again.

She got down the stairs. She held on to Adam's hand and he took her round to her front door and opened it with her key. 'Good night,' she said. 'Can I give you a lift into the office in the morning? Oh, silly me, it's Sunday.'

'Just shut up and go to bed,' he said. He put her inside the hall and closed the front door behind her, and she reached for the light switch but stopped before she pressed it. That would wake her parents, and she didn't want to talk any more tonight.

She crept upstairs and into her bedroom, undressing in the dim light that filtered through the window. She didn't want to see anyone, especially herself. Perhaps she was asleep already and none of it had happened.

She woke during the night with an aching head and a raging thirst, so that she had to go to the bathroom and get a glass of water, but she was nowhere up to facing up to what she had done. She took two aspirins from the medicine cupboard and swallowed them, then crawled back to bed, and it hardly mattered that she had made such a fool of herself when she was feeling so rotten that she could well be dying.

But it mattered next time she woke. Her headache was beating like a steel band inside her skull, but she was cold sober. Her mother stood beside the bed holding a cup of tea and asking brightly, 'Was it a good party?'

'I drank too much,' said Annie.

'That was silly.' Catrin could never remember that happening before. She put the tea beside the bed and began to pick up Annie's clothes, which were scattered all around. 'I've got something to tell you.'

'Adam's in the loft.'

'You know?' Annie was lying very still with her eyes closed. 'Now don't be annoyed. I knew you'd object and I didn't know that he'd agree, but I don't really use it, it was wasted space. This way it's earning, and we can always use the money.'

Annie said nothing. Her mother put her skirt and blouse over one chair, her undies on another, and set her shoes neatly together. 'Your father asked him last night if he was interested and it seems he was going to start looking around for a small flat, so wasn't that lucky? He came over and he took it right away, he only went back for his luggage. How did you know?'

'I saw the light on,' Annie explained. 'He was still working. He gave me a cup of coffee.'

'That was nice.' Annie hadn't the strength to argue. She heard the door closing before she could say, 'Not really. I lurched in and asked him to make love to me and he threw me out.'

Not that she could ever say that, but it was what had happened, and heaven knows what Adam was thinking about them all. He liked the bedsitter, which would probably be convenient for him, but he knew that her parents were after a man for Annie. He wasn't letting that bother him, it seemed, but that was before Annie had arrived after midnight, making him an offer he could and did refuse.

He would surely believe now that she was in the know about luring him here as a lodger. She'd *told* him she had designs on him. Maybe he would lock his door after this, to stop her popping up again in the small hours.

Shame scalded her. She hauled herself into a sitting position and made herself drink her tea. She had to apologise. Sorry, she had to say, it won't happen again. I don't know what came over me. She hadn't wanted him to know how she felt, going overboard for a man she'd known less than a week. But if she said, 'It wasn't personal, I was just babbling, I don't have a crush on you,' then she might as well be saying, 'I'm easy, I would have slept with any presentable man,' and that was utterly untrue.

She was only a fool over Adam. She had wanted him, desperately and crazily. She had never before asked a man if she could stay the night with him, or begged, 'Love me.'

Why hadn't he let her stay? She would have been quiet. She would have slept on that divan, curled up, taking very little room so that he could have slept too. She wouldn't have disturbed him. And this morning she could have said, 'I have the most terrible head. Was I terrible last night? But I do have a crush on you, I do think you're special. I'm sorry I was a nuisance.'

It would have been all right if he had laughed. She would have deserved that and she would have tried to laugh at herself. But she was here, alone, feeling sick and ashamed and oh, so stupid to have done such a damn fool thing.

The phone rang, and when it stopped ringing her father called, 'Annie, it's Robert Marsden!'

It hurt her head to shout, 'Tell him I'm asleep!'

'He seems very anxious to speak to you.'

She crawled out of bed, and into a towelling robe that had hung behind the door. Holding this round her, she stumbled downstairs and picked up the phone that her father had left on the hall table. 'Hello.' she croaked.

'Annie? Are you all right?'

'Of course I am.' It was as well that TV phones were not being installed, because her image in the mirror just over the table was a mess. Last night's mascara was smudged into great black shadows, and her golden tan had turned yellowish.

Robert said, 'They told me you'd gone with Carl and Christina, but I was worried about you.'

'Why?' The party had been swinging when she left, she had been no merrier than most.

'Well, you were pretty high. You got home all right?'

'They brought me to the gate. There's not a lot can happen to you between your front gate and your front door.' Unless you go to somebody else's door first, of course. 'But I do have a bit of a headache this morning, so thank you for ringing, and I'm going back to bed.'

'When shall I see——?' he was asking as she put the phone down.

She was halfway up the stairs when her father asked from the hall, 'Have a good time?'

'I reckon so,' she said. She didn't turn round, she would rather he didn't get a good look at her. 'What time is it?'

'About half eleven.'

Annie went to the bathroom and removed the residue of her make-up, then she washed her face in cold water, splashing her temples and her hair. It was refreshing, and she swallowed two more aspirins, and took down the first dress that came to hand in the wardrobe. She was only wearing one earring. She slipped that out, replacing it with small gold studs, then went downstairs, with her sunglasses perched on the end of her nose, because the sun was shining and it was altogether too bright for comfort.

Her mother was singing softly, with the radio in the kitchen, in a sweet true voice, and Annie went into the lounge and picked up a newspaper. She wasn't reading it. She was hiding behind it, hoping she would feel better soon and that, before she saw Adam, she would think of something to say that would blot out everything she had said to him last night.

Keeping out of his way might be cowardly, but it was the best idea she was coming up with.

The phone rang again and she tried not to hear it, but she heard her mother say, 'Yes, yes, I'll call him. Eunice. Yes.'

Please, prayed Annie, don't let him tell Eunice. Not that he was likely to, on the hall phone. On another phone perhaps, or when they met, and it would be no more than Eunice expected. She would have shut the door and put her hands over her ears, but she felt that she would still hear him talking.

As she stood behind the curtains, looking through the french windows, she saw Adam walking with her mother towards the house, and heard herself whimper. She really was in the most idiotic state! As soon as they came into the house, through the kitchen door, she shot across the lawn, heading for the farthest recess of the garden, and the old stone seat.

Eunice had wasted no time in phoning here. She wondered what Eunice had to say about Adam moving into Annie's home. 'That girl is waiting for the chance to make a complete fool of herself over you.' 'Funny you should say that,' Adam might reply.

He might not have been looking for Annie, he might just have been walking round the garden, but a few minutes later he came. 'Good morning,' he said.

She was glad she was wearing sunglasses, they hid her

eyes. She wished she had been wearing a big hat that would have hidden her face. He sat down beside her, and she had to say something. 'I'm sure it is,' she said, 'but I'm not up to meeting it head-on just yet.'

She heard him chuckle and she took a deep breath and plunged on. 'About last night—I've been trying to think what I should say to you, but I haven't come up with anything very brilliant.'

She scuffed the toe of her shoe on a flagstone. There were coloured slabs among the grey, pale green, pale pink, blue. When it rained the colours were quite bright, but the summer had been so dry that they all looked the same now, under a coating of dust. Annie had loved the hot summer, but today she wished it would rain. Her head was aching and she felt stifled.

She couldn't look at Adam, not even from behind the dark glasses. She kept her eyes down. 'I could have said I couldn't remember, that didn't seem a bad idea and believe me, I wish it was true. Or that after a few drinks that's the way I usually carry on. Only it isn't. I've never made such a fool of myself before.'

She was mumbling, but he could hear her and she blurted, 'What I said about having a crush on you is true. I've never met anyone like you.'

'You mean you've never met another man you didn't snare on sight?' He wasn't taking it seriously, and that had to be a relief. But of course it wasn't serious to him.

'Of course I have,' she said. 'I was just trying to say that if you'd find it embarrassing, living in the loft, after last night . . .'

'No, I don't think so.' It would take more than Annie confessing a crush, to embarrass Adam Corbett. He produced her earring from his pocket, and offered it to her, and she took it gingerly, avoiding brushing his fingers.

'Where did you find it?' she asked.

'In my bed.'

'Well, I'm certainly glad you picked it up before my mother came over. If she'd seen it there she might have expected you to make an honest woman of me.' The only thing to do was joke. 'You think I'm such a ninny, don't you?' she said, and she was horribly scared that she might start to cry.

'I think you're very talented, very attractive,' said Adam. 'I can understand why most of the men you meet fall for you.' Annie's heart gave a little leap. He was serious now, looking straight at her, and he touched her cheek; but the touch was not loverlike although it was gentle and light. 'But if I were your father,' he told her, 'I should wish you were a little more circumspect in your dealings with some of them.'

'How old are you?' she demanded.

'Thirty-four.'

'I'm going on twenty-three, so how the hell could you be my father? She knew what he meant, though, that she acted like a spoiled and precocious child rather than an adult. She thought it likely that her mother had been telling him about the nice young men that Annie had unaccountably left in the lurch. 'But I'm not usually so irresponsible, and all right, my conduct last night was not exactly circumspect,' she exaggerated the word, drawling it, 'but—only once did I really let someone down. It was a long time ago, I let things get out of hand, but it taught me a lesson. That was when I nearly got married.'

'Yes.' So he did know about that, and she asked,

'Have you ever been married?'

'No.'

'Ever come near?' He knew too much about her. All she knew about him was that he was brilliant and successful, had nearly got himself killed six months ago, and she had a terrible premonition that she could never let any other man touch her.

'Mine isn't the kind of life for marriage,' he said. His

life wasn't here. He would need a very jet-set sort of woman as his partner, and she asked, 'Not even Eunice?' She hadn't wanted to say anything about Eunice. She certainly didn't want to add, 'I suppose you know her very well?'

And she deserved the answer she got. 'Very well—we lived together.' And that should teach her to think before she spoke, because that was like a hard slap across the face, and she wasn't sure whether he'd said 'lived' or 'live'. The relationship was flourishing, dinners and phone calls and at least one overnight stay, but was there a house that they shared, between his travels? Would he go back there when he left here? Where was it? Oh, what could he *see* in Eunice?

She managed to smile and say lightly, 'That must be a marriage of true minds.'

'We get on well.' She wouldn't let that sink in, that Adam and Eunice were right for each other. If she did she would begin thinking of the ways in which a man and a woman could be right, and she wanted to scream, 'No!'

She said, 'You make a very distinguished pair. Everybody turned to look when you walked out of the dining room together. It's both being so tall, I think. You get taken seriously if you're up there looking down. I bet if I was six inches taller I'd get more respect. She's very serious, isn't she—Eunice?'

'Most of the time,' said Adam.

Eunice Fleming's books were serious all the time, there was never a laugh in them. 'And very circumspect,' said Annie. 'I'll bet you could take her anywhere.'

He laughed and shook his head. 'I find it very hard to believe that I'm not old enough to be your father,' he said, and she shut her mouth. Then she said, 'I talk too much.' Words had always come fluently to her—talking, writing. Sometimes she used them as a smokescreen to hide her feelings if she was unhappy or tired or worried. That was what she had been doing this morning. Now she wasn't concentrating on talking or trying to smile the pain in her temples throbbed, although it was nothing compared with the leaden ache in her chest.

After a little while she asked, 'Would you know a cure for headache?'

'Quietness,' said Adam.

It was quiet out here, except for the faint hum of insects. The birds overhead skimmed on silent wings, and not a leaf stirred. Her muscles had stiffened when she saw him coming, all the time they were talking she had been uptight, but now she felt the tension draining out of her. When it was so quiet you couldn't breathe shallowly, that would give you away. You had to take deep quiet breaths and you had to relax. Her arm was against his arm, her bare skin against the coat sleeve, but she felt his strength flowing into her and she let her head droop on to his shoulder. She wasn't thinking of anything, just giving herself over to a sensation that was like floating on one of the fluffy little white clouds.

She didn't want to open her eyes, nor move, nor speak. She wanted to sit here all day, all night, and it was probably a good ten minutes before she did open her eyes. Then she smiled, 'It's better.'

'Good.'

'Are you having lunch with us?'

He was eating out, he said. Eunice, she thought, and that brought her off cloud nine and back to reality. As they walked towards the loft and the house they passed her father, who was frowing up at the sky, and asked them, 'Do they look like rain clouds to you?'

'No,' said Adam.

'It's got to break before long,' said Douglas Bennett.

'Of course it has,' said Annie, who had been doing

most of the watering for weeks. At the door of the shed that led to the loft she said, 'Friends?'

'I should hope so,' said Adam, and she said, 'Then that's all right,' and told herself, It's a start. We're closer than we were. I sat with my head on his shoulder and he's living here. But if he should ever bring Eunice back I don't know how I should cope.

She did not know. He had told her they lived together and she couldn't think of that without black boiling jealousy. But if she knew that Adam and Eunice were alone, where she could see from her bedroom window when the glow of their light went out, that might be too much for her to bear and she might just go to pieces.

The news that Adam Corbett had moved into the Bennetts' loft meant that Annie got a few funny looks in the office. 'Was this your idea?' Charlie wanted to know, and he wasn't the only one wondering that.

Megan asked her and Annie said, honestly, that there was nothing between them. Eunice was ringing him, he lived with Eunice. While he was in Llanaven he was living in the studio, using the bathroom in the house but nothing else. He didn't eat with the family, he didn't sit with them. He didn't even come into the office in Annie's car. He took a taxi, night and morning, and in the office Annie saw him no more than the rest of the staff.

In the office his dynamic presence made everything and everybody move quicker. The week started as it went on, even routine stories were tackled with a new enthusiasm.

On Tuesday evening Annie heard the typing from the loft as she watered the roses. She had wanted to go up there last night, but shyness had stopped her. She was a girl with deeper reserves than anyone guessed, but she had never been shy before. Her father had said, 'I wonder if Adam would like to come over for a nightcap?' looking at Annie, and Annie had said, 'Why don't you ask him?'

'I thought you might.'

But she couldn't get up and go and invite Adam over here, although she wished desperately that her father would. 'I'd rather not,' she said, and went on hoping he would come until it was bedtime.

On Tuesday evening when she heard the typing she put down the watering can and ran quickly up the steps before her inhibitions could stop her. The door at the top was ajar and she put her head in and asked, 'Could you use a typist?'

She was probably disturbing a flow of ideas, but he smiled. 'Not yet, I'm thinking, not writing.' She sidled through the door and he said, 'Come in.'

'Am I disturbing you?'

'No.' That was good, because it meant she could stay a while, but he disturbed her. Her entire nervous system jangled when she looked at him, and she would have given years of her life for him to come and put his arms around her. She sat in a basketwork chair, Adam sat in the hide armchair.

But she was in the room. She was doing all right as a friend, and she had a glass of wine and they talked.

She felt a little like a kitten allowed in because it's friendly and amusing. If Adam touched her at all, she felt, it would be to stroke her head, but she hoped he wouldn't. If he did she might reach for his hand and hold on to it, and she wasn't going to make that kind of a fool of herself again.

He didn't touch her, but she stayed for the rest of the evening. She asked about his book and was flattered when he explained what it would be about—fact and fiction combined, set behind the Iron Curtain in the dark world of secret police. He knew what he was writing about, and Annie shivered in the warm little room, thinking how terrible it would be to be followed and spied on.

She didn't want to go, but of course she had to get up at last and say, 'I'd better go home.' It was less than a minute's walk, but really it was a great divide, the difference between going and staying, and she had no hope that Adam would ever ask her to stay. 'Good night,' she said now, at the top of the steps going down from the loft.

'Watch it,' said Adam. The steps were steep, and she was skipping down, looking back at him rather than where she was going. And she had slipped on the patio that first morning. But she joked now,

'That's all right, I never slip unless there's someone to catch me.'

'Very sensible,' he said.

She walked out into the garden. The lights from the loft and the house made the lawn bright where she crossed, but before she went in through the kitchen door she looked back again, her eyes straining to pierce the surrounding darkness. This must be how it was for the men and women Adam was writing about, this prickling apprehension. She was either identifying with them or getting a complex about shadows.

She went across next evening, not too early, and stayed for half an hour. She told him that she had ambitions to write a book herself some day, and he told her to get started, and the thought of them both writing their books through the winter months was a pleasant little fantasy, reading each other's work before anybody else saw it. But it was as unlikely as Adam becoming her lover. He would never need her professional advice any more than he would need her. And she wouldn't feel like showing him her attempts at fiction, because look at the competition she was up against. Eunice, who was reviewed in the Sunday literary supplements, most of whom said she was terrific.

Catrin was pleased with the way things were going. Although Adam kept to himself he and Annie were spending more time together and that was a good sign. Friday evening Catrin suggested that Annie asked him to have lunch with the family on Sunday. Usually he ate before he returned in the evenings, or brought back convenience food. It was still hot, not the weather for heavy cooked meals, but Annie tapped on the door and called, 'It's only me. Can I come in?'

She always timed it so that he had had some time for work. This was the fourth evening, and he seemed pleased to see her, as though she was the neighbourly kitten, dropping in for a saucer of milk. She had been allowed to curl up on one of his chairs and purr away, and on the outside she was a kitten; and if he had known that it would have taken only a word or a touch to turn her into a tiger she probably wouldn't have been allowed in here again because he wasn't wanting a tiger around. Not one called Annie, anyway.

'By the way,' she said, 'message from my mother. Will you have dinner with us on Sunday? Or lunch or whatever you call it.'

He said he would have liked that, but he would be away for the weekend. He was going to London on Saturday and coming back on Monday morning.

'Anothe time, then,' said Annie.

She wanted to ask, 'Are you going home to Eunice? What kind of place do you share?' She had thought a lot about that home, visualising it as a penthouse flat, very modern and elegant, with abstract paintings and Design Centre furniture; and the idea of Adam arriving there tomorrow and Eunice welcoming him made her clench her hands so that her nails cut into her palms.

She didn't ask him anything. She said, 'I'm going water-skiing tomorrow,' and that sounded busy and bright as if her weekend would be as eventful as his. He wouldn't know that this evening hour was the highlight of her day and that she was feeling as bereft as if he was sailing away for months.

'Adam won't be here over the weekend, so he can't come to dinner on Sunday,' she told her mother later, and Catrin, sipping her hot milk, said that was a pity. Her father was listening to the weather forecast and viewing the charts hopefully. 'See that,' he said. 'It looks as if it's finally breaking up.'

'What is?' asked Annie.

'The drought—the summer. And not before time. When the rain does come, mark my words, it will be a deluge.'

Prolonged heatwaves usually ended in storms, but before that weekend ended his words were going to have a ring of bitter prophecy. Because for Annie the summer was already over. Around her the dark clouds were gathering.

She did not see Adam next day. He went into the office early and it was a day off for Annie. Not much editorial work was done on Saturday, he would probably be on his way to London by midday.

She could have gone water-skiing. She had friends with speedboats who would be zooming around the coastline, although the temperature had dropped this morning. She had no firm plans. She had fobbed off Robert and she was aimless this weekend without Adam, although she knew that was no way to be.

After breakfast she went shopping in town with her mother, for provisions mostly. Annie carried the bags, because Douglas Bennett disliked shopping and nobody ever mentioned that he could no longer manage heavy weights. Annie enjoyed wandering around the supermarket and popping into the baker's and the delicatessen, and she didn't mind staggering back to the car loaded like a pack mule.

Then as they passed Germaine's her mother spotted a dress and jacket in the window and said, 'Now that's just what I've been looking for.'

Annie had to admit it was nice. In blue, which was her mother's favourite colour and reasonably priced for the priciest dress shop in town. Annie never went into Mrs Lloyd Williams' shop herself, it was not aimed at the younger budget-conscious woman, but even if it had been she knew that David's mother did not want her or her custom.

Her mother was welcome. Catrin Bennett had been distraught when the wedding was cancelled at the last minute, nobody could blame Catrin.

Mrs Lloyd Williams still nurtured a king-size grudge against Annie, and Annie put down the two heavy shopping bags while her mother looked at the suit a little longer, then picked them up reluctantly to follow her mother into the shop.

An assistant came forward, to be waved away by Germaine, who greeted Catrin effusively, ignoring Annie. The suit was taken out of the window and Germaine asked how Douglas was keeping, and when Catrin enquired after her family said, 'Oh, we're all fine. David's doing well. He and his wife are very happy. She's a lovely girl, he thinks the world of her. Hello, Anna, you're looking pale, are you well?'

Annie hadn't thought she was pale, but the bags were heavy and she had carried them a fair way, and Mrs Lloyd Williams always managed to make her feel guilty.

Her mother went to try on the suit behind an ivory velvet curtain in a cubicle, and as Annie put down her bags again Mrs Lloyd Williams said, 'Not married yet, I see. It was Huw Sanders, wasn't it? Is that all over? But of course you've always been very hard to please, I sometimes wonder what kind of man you *are* waiting for, it wouldn't surprise me if you ended up an old maid.'

'Wouldn't it?' said Annie, and she turned, raising her voice to ask, 'How does it look? Can I see?' and she stepped through the curtain and pulled up the back zipper that her mother was struggling with.

If Mrs Lloyd Williams had known that Annie was caught at last, hopelessly enmeshed by a man who didn't want her, that would have made her day. Once out of this shop, thought Annie, and wild horses will never drag me in again.

'What do you think?' asked her mother, smoothing the dress down over her hips and smiling. 'Should I, do you think?' She sought Annie's reflection in the mirror for encouragement and stared at it, 'Are you all right?' She swung her head round. 'You're looking——'

'Pale,' and Annie managed a grin. 'It's the coming storm Dad keeps threatening us with. You have the suit—it's lovely. I'll see you outside.'

Her mother decided the bags were too heavy, and they carried one each the rest of the way to the car park. But Annie's 'faint turn' meant that she wasn't badgered about going out this evening. She sat with them, watching television, until Douglas decided to go to bed early. He said there was nothing else he wanted to see, but his wife gave him an anxious look. A drizzle of rain had started to fall mid-afternoon and he had been breaking up the crust of earth to help it reach the roots. Now he was tired, although that was natural enough. Catrin had a library book and she said she wouldn't mind an early night herself, so just after ten o'clock Annie stood alone in the kitchen wondering what she could take to knock her out till morning.

Tonight would be filled with images of Adam and Eunice, and she dreaded going up to her own bed, and lying there while the pictures kept unfolding in her mind. Her mother had sleeping pills that she took occasionally and kept in her bedroom. If they had been in any other room Annie would have helped herself to a couple and risked a heavy head tomorrow.

It was early yet. Adam and Eunice might be out on

the town. Or perhaps Eunice would have fixed a meal in their flat. Annie wondered if she might possibly be telepathic, because she could visualise that flat so clearly. She stared out of the kitchen window into a starless night and saw a candlelit table, the shadows falling on Adam's tough uncompromising face, eyes piercing the way they did when he listened with that intense undivided attention. And then the smile that softened the harshness. That was the best Annie had had, the smile, but tonight he would be looking at Eunice in another way, and Annie pressed her fingertips to her temples and thought—if I am psychic I'd like to haunt that flat for five minutes. No longer. I don't want to be a ghost in the night, I don't want to see them in the night. But right now I'd like to upturn the table or crash a few saucepans or ring a fire alarm.

Or a phone bell. She could imagine the phone, one of the modern press-button kind with a very discreet ring, and she closed her eyes and tried to read the number. Then she opened them again and wondered if she *was* flipping, although it might be interesting to ring what she thought she saw and see what happened.

No, it wouldn't be interesting, it would be daft, but the idea of phoning was interesting. If she did know his number she would. That might break the mood and rile Eunice. 'How did you get my number?' Adam would ask, and the only way she might get it would be by going over to the loft and looking for it. Although the odds were against him writing down his own number. It might of course be Eunice's. If she did track him down she would say, 'I'm a reporter, aren't I?' and go on talking and leave the explanation until he got back.

What else would she say? 'I'm sick with jealousy. My life has never been in such a mess. What am I going to do?' But of course she couldn't say that. She might say, 'Just thought I'd like to say goodnight. I've been saying good night to you most of the week and it's becoming a habit.' Or maybe, 'Sorry to bother you, but you know what that man said, about Jud Dane sending somebody after me? Well, I know he's finished at the nightclub now and I suppose they've all gone, but I have had a weird feeling lately that I'm being followed. I went out to post a letter tonight and I got it again. I'm beginning to get scared.'

It wasn't true that she was scared, but she did have a feeling almost certainly due to Adam's book, because Jud Dane's P.R. had known it would be worse than stupid to take revenge on Annie for that bad publicity. But she would go over to the loft, and if she found the number she would take it from there.

There were two keys. Adam had one, the other was in a drawer in the kitchen, and Annie took a torch and let herself out of the house very quietly, running across the lawn and opening the loft door. As soon as she was inside the room she felt better, although there was no reason why she should. Adam was still with Eunice, she was still alone, but here she felt closer to him. If she only put on the desk lamp she could almost fool herself that he was here. 'Hello,' she said.

The drawers in the desk were where he kept his papers, but she couldn't go rooting through them. If she found a London number she wouldn't know if that was the one, and he would be angry if she started ringing around after him. She had never seen him angry, but she had no doubt that if need arose he could blast all before him, and that could include her if she opened one of those drawers.

Besides, it wasn't hard to imagine that he was in that chair. If she didn't look directly at it she could sit in her usual chair and talk to him, telling him about Mrs Lloyd Williams this morning. She would have done that tonight if he had been here, making a joke of it, but now she told it the way it was, full of cold malice, and she thought Adam might have said, 'Don't worry about it. You were too young, you didn't love him.' She had told her parents that when she realised she could not go through with it and Catrin had said that the love would have come.

And it had, three years later, for another man. If she had married David, and then met Adam, she would still be feeling this way now. 'I never fell in love until I met you,' she said, 'and if I was writing a story I'd have a tape recorder running somewhere so that when you come back you'd hear all this and be glad about it. Unless of course the story was going to have a dreary ending like one of Eunice's. What *do* you see in Eunice?'

She sat quietly for a while, feeling Adam's presence in the room because this was where he lived. It was his desk, his chair, his bed.

'May I stay tonight?' she asked.

Of course, he said, and she switched off the lamp and kicked off her shoes and lay under the coverlet. There still wasn't a star in the sky when she looked up through the skylight, but when she closed her eyes she could imagine he would be coming soon. Now he was moving quietly round the room, soon he would touch her, and she would open her arms and he would hold her closer, closer.

She wouldn't open her eyes again. She would lie here dreaming and maybe he would come. For some reason perhaps he would leave London and come back tonight, and arrive at two or three or four, and she would be waiting. That, she knew, was sheer wishful thinking, but Adam's bed lulled her to sleep as her own could not have done, and it was daylight when she woke.

She checked on her earrings; it would be hard to explain if she left another one around. Then she smoothed the bed. She had done no harm, she had hardly touched a thing, but she would rather nobody knew she had been here all night. She went back to the house, tiptoeing upstairs. Her parents were still sleeping, and she undressed, bathed and put on a warm dress. After the long hot weeks the unaccustomed chill of this morning seemed to strike to her bones.

The rain was coming down in a heavy mist and the outlook was miserable. If the sun had still been shining she would have made an effort to do something, go somewhere, but all she really wanted to do was sit in her room and wait for tomorrow and Adam.

She made herself cook breakfast and help prepare lunch. She kept up her usual bright façade for her mother and father, until the phone rang while she was washing up after the midday meal and her mother came into the kitchen to say, 'That was Germaine Lloyd Williams. You'll never guess what I did yesterday—I wrote the wrong year on that cheque. The wrong *year*! I don't know what I was thinking of.'

Annie probably, who had gone out of the shop looking pale, blaming it on the weather. 'She's bringing it round,' Annie's mother said. 'I've asked them to tea. I've just got time to make a walnut cake.'

'I'll be out,' said Annie.

'There's no need——'

Oh, but there was; Annie had never been so vulnerable to Mrs Lloyd Williams' barbs and jibes. David's mother and father hadn't been round here since the night Annie stopped the wedding, but that was over three years ago, and Germaine had always been 'all right' with Catrin. Her mother could see no reason why Annie should not hand round the sandwiches and the walnut cake. David was happily married, and Annie was getting on so well with Adam.

If her mother mentioned that Mrs Lloyd Williams would have a field day, probing, digging, saying hypocritically, 'Well, I do hope this time will be different. Is he serious about Anna? Has he asked her to marry him?'

As soon as she had finished the washing up Annie climbed into her car, switching on the windscreen wipers and getting away. She thought she would walk somewhere she was not likely to meet anyone, and come back after the visitors had left, tired enough to sleep tonight in her own bed.

She drove up into the hills, parking her car under the trees by the trackside, and scrambling through the rough grass up to the caves. The Romans and the Normans had mined here for copper and lead, but it was the myth of Merlin that had fascinated Annie when she was a child. The thought of the old Welsh wizard in his enchanted sleep had taken her miles from home when she was young enough to believe.

Sometimes she had walked, sometimes she had cycled, but her parents had never realised just how far she did range, all alone. They were over-protective from the start and she had slipped early into subterfuge. Even as a child not much had scared her.

But it was a long time since she had taken this particular walk. The caves didn't change. She came at last to the place, deep in the hillside, where she had heard the 'breathing' through the high and narrow crack that she had been convinced led to the crystal cave. She wouldn't get through there now, although she was small and agile, but as a child she had managed to squirm through. It led to another cave, and as she had stumbled around in there she had dropped her torch.

Now that had been terror, the sound of it rolling away, and then such blackness. She had screamed once, her voice echoing around her, and then she had searched for the torch on hands and knees and she had known that if she did find it and it was broken, even if she could find the crack in the rocks again, she could still be lost in the heart of the hills, where no one would look for her.

But she had found the torch and it had worked. Now

at least she was wiser, inasmuch as she had a spare torch in her pocket and a box of matches, and she would have to find her own way through the darkness and loneliness of life without Adam because, again, there was no help coming.

And this was a gloomy place to walk with the miseries. She couldn't go back home until she was sure the Lloyd Williams had gone, but she could call on friends, where it would be warm and dry and she could try to be cheerful. Megan's maybe, she could drop in on Megan and Barny anytime.

The rain was heavier when she came out of the caves, this would be pleasing her father. She turned up her collar and hurried down towards the clump of trees where she had left her car. The sky was black. So were the trees, dripping with rain. Annie's little red Triumph made a splash of colour, but she didn't notice the black car parked under the trees until she was almost on it.

She took off her mac and tossed it on to the back seat, and then she saw the other car door open and a man got out; and suddenly she knew who had been watching her from the shadows.

CHAPTER SIX

I'M dying, she thought. She smelled petrol and she lay twisted and trapped in her little car. Without moving her head she could see shattered glass, silvered like a web, and through a gaping hole grass where the sky should be. Something heavy held her down, but she felt no pain, no sensation.

Adam, she thought. I'm leaving Adam; and she struggled to stay alive, although she was not moving a muscle, nor making a sound, although she thought she was screaming his name. It was all a nightmare, jagged and jumbled. She was lifted and then there was pain. She heard a siren, then something was clamped over her face and she tried to twist her head away. She asked once, 'What happened?' and one of the swimming faces mouthed at her as she spiralled down into the pit.

She didn't know what they were doing to her. Once she felt a tweak on her earlobe and a pressure over her eyes. Blinding lights came at her. and as suddenly it was dark. She was out of this world in a world of shadowy forms and shifting images and pain, until there was no pain and time ceased to be . . .

She could only open her eyes to slits, but that was enough to have the night nurse bending over her. She was lying flat and a knife went through her when she breathed. 'What happened to me?' she whispered.

'You had a little accident.'

The car, she remembered, and she was so tired that all she could do was close her eyes again.

'Your mother's here,' somebody said softly hours later, but it was Megan she saw first, beside the bed.

'Oh, you poor love!' whispered Megan. 'Those

bloody brakes!' Her mother was there, grey-faced and red-eyed, and Annie said, 'Sorry.'

She knew she was drugged. She knew she was injured. One arm, lying beside her, was in plaster from hand to elbow, the other was bandaged. Her face felt peculiar, everything about her felt weird, and she wanted to sleep and she wanted her mother to stop crying. 'Where's my father?' she whispered.

'He's gone home,' said Megan. 'They've been here all night, I'll take her home now—Sister said we must only stay a minute.' Megan was smiling a strange strained smile, and they were both moving back.

'Megan,' Annie managed to get the words out, 'tell Adam to bring my father.'

She was woken every half hour, she learned later, while they took her blood pressure, pulse and temperature. Once she was given a sip of water, and when the tea trolley came round at eight o'clock there was a softly spoken discussion as to whether or not she should be allowed a cup of tea.

She wanted one. Her mouth was dry. She said, 'Yes, please,' and they raised her head, and she swallowed and winced at the pain in her chest and asked, 'Could I have a pillow?' but the pillow was so flat it made no difference.

The doctor came. She had always known Dr Parry, he didn't seem to have changed in twenty-odd years. He had always had longish grey hair and he usually looked harassed. He was looking worried now, checking her chart at the foot of the bed. 'This could have been a very nasty business,' he told her.

'Isn't it?' Her lips felt blubbery.

'You'll live. But you should have been wearing a seat belt.'

She always did. He shone a light into her eyes and she wondered what he could see down there; she asked, 'Is my father all right?'

He frowned, 'What?'

'My father. This would be a shock for him.'

'It was a shock for both of them, but they're all right.' She thought he hesitated. Shock and stress were the last things her father needed with his heart condition, and when the phone call came or the knock on the door, and they were told that Annie had crashed her car, anything could have happened. They could be keeping it from her because she was in such a battered state herself, waiting until she was stronger to tell her.

She was sedated, but she was conscious enough to recognise that she was in a ward of six beds in the Cottage Hospital. She had visited friends in here. Some of the other beds were occupied, but she was too weak to look around. She lay with closed eyes, her fears for her father only out of her mind while she slept, and even then still disturbing her on all but the deepest level of unconsciousness. She took medicines, but no one was telling her the extent of her injuries. The nurses were cheerful, tending her, and she was in no state to demand details. She was more concerned about her father than about herself, although she could be disfigured, crippled. When she managed to touch her face it seemed like a balloon, monstrously swollen. She could move her toes and she could feel her fingers, but there was this pain when she breathed as though something was terribly wrong.

She heard Adam coming, the tap of his walking stick, and she knew how awful she must look, but he was the person in the world she most wanted here. Then he was looking down at her. 'What the blazes have you been doing to yourself?' he demanded.

A nurse was just behind him, and although Annie could hardly see through her puffy eyelids she could see how Nurse Evans was looking at Adam. She added, 'Has my father had another heart attack?'

Adam kept his eyes on her. 'Yes,' he said.

'Is he——?' She couldn't go on, but his voice and his eyes were steady.

'It isn't serious. Better not let him see you in this state, but you will see him soon.'

Adam she believed. She knew that he would tell her the truth, and she said tremulously, 'Oh God, I worry about them. If anything happened to my father my mother would be finished. Please take care of them for me until I get out of here.'

'Of course.'

'Is my face an awful mess?'

He smiled, and that was such a relief that she tried to smile too, although with her lips so swollen it could have only been a grimace. 'You could have done several rounds in a boxing ring,' he said, 'but there's no permanent damage.'

'What else?'

'Well, you broke an arm, cracked a couple of ribs and collected some cuts and bruises.'

'Is that all?'

'Isn't that enough? Why weren't you wearing a seat-belt?'

'I don't know,' she said slowly, 'I don't remember anything about it. Where was I going?'

'Does it matter?'

'No.' She was going to be strong and pretty again, and her father would be all right, and that was what mattered.

'She needs to sleep,' said the nurse.

'I'll see you later.' He stooped to kiss her cheek and the nurse asked, 'Did you feel that?'

Annie would have laughed if she could, because she was not sure whether she had literally felt Adam's lips against her numbed face, but she did know that when he bent over and kissed her she was wrapped in such comfort that nothing had hurt any more. 'I think I felt it,' she said.

The flowers arrived within the hour. 'My goodness, you are popular!' said Sister. 'We're going to be running out of vases at this rate. Somebody must have bought the flower shop!'

It could have been all her colleagues, Megan was capable of taking up an immediate collection, but Sister read the card, 'From one crock to another,' and Annie thought, Maybe it's worth it. He kissed me and bought me a flower shop. She could only half open her eyes and it hurt to move her head, but she could see the blaze of colour and smell the fragrance. 'Please put a rose by me,' she said. 'A red one.'

Her tests were hourly now, and they were in something of a quandary. She had a frontal bump on her head bad enough to bruise and swell her face almost out of recognition, so she should have been lying flat. But the fractured ribs made breathing agonising, it would have been a little easier if she could have been propped up. So long as there were no signs of brain damage she would be tomorrow, but she passed the day lying flat and feeling like death, but knowing how close she had come to death and how much she wanted to live and watching the red rose. When she wasn't sleeping because she had never felt so tired.

It was evening before she was allowed visitors again. She didn't want them before. The other patients had visitors during the afternoon who talked and laughed, and Annie was so glad they weren't around her bed. She resented being disturbed for the tests, and when meals were brought round she took a little soup, but it tasted foul, and it wasn't food she craved, only sleep.

She had to make an effort for her mother, who must be worried sick what with Annie and her father, and they propped her up a little for the evening visiting hour, bathed her face, which stung and throbbed, and brushed her hair very gently. She must look awful and soon she would hate Adam to see her like this, but today her need was stronger than her pride. Besides, he had already seen her, so it would be no shock for him.

Adam might not come again today. She had friends galore who had known her longer and thought they were closer; and her mother had friends galore who would rally to support her and ferry her. But when she saw him she felt she had known he would come.

Her mother was carrying flowers and trying to smile, but when she reached the bed her lips began to tremble and she gave up all pretence and her face clenched on silent sobs. Adam put her into a chair and sat down beside her, and Annie saw how she dropped the flowers and reached for his hands. 'She's going to be all right,' he said. 'As good as new in no time.'

'Thank you for all these flowers,' croaked Annie. 'They're lovely. How long am I going to be a crock?'

'Not long, if you behave yourself.' He stooped to pick up the bunch of sweet peas her mother had dropped. 'Your father sent you these.'

'Honestly?' Even if her father had asked someone else to gather them from the garden it was still a good sign.

'And a note.' Adam took that from his pocket and held it for her to read. The writing was firm and she recognised it. 'One good thing about this is that car is a write-off. Your mother is waiting to say, "I told you so". Come home soon, Love, Dad.'

'Bless you,' she said. She knew Adam had suggested her father send a note with the flowers to reassure her. She said, so quietly that her mother didn't catch it, 'I thought I'd killed him.'

'You nearly killed yourself! No belt, no brakes—you shouldn't be let out!'

A flicker of gaiety rose in her. 'Don't bully me. Pick on someone your own size!'

Annie's mother was pulling herself together. It had been the most dreadful night of her life. Douglas had had a seizure while they waited in the hospital for news of Annie. They had kept him overnight and this morning he had been allowed home, with instructions to be sensible and take it easy.

The news of Annie's crash had been all over the town, not long after it happened, and Megan and Barry had driven out to the hospital. Megan had stayed. She had been here when Douglas had slumped from his chair, spilling the cup of cold tea he had been holding, and she had supported Catrin through the night.

Catrin was glad Douglas hadn't seen Annie, at five o'clock this morning when they let her and Megan into the ward. Because if he had seen his beautiful daughter, lying so helpless, her poor face disfigured, it might have brought on a more massive heart attack.

She could hardly believe that Annie was not permanently disfigured. Not even when Adam told her that he had talked with doctors and staff. He was no kin, but he was Adam Corbett; they knew him, or knew of him, and he got answers. From when Adam returned this morning he had taken charge, and Catrin had stopped crying until she walked into the ward just now and saw Annie again.

But Adam was smiling and he must have sent Annie all these flowers, and Annie was trying to joke while Catrin gave herself a little shake and tried to remember some of the names of people who had phoned.

'And I'm to collect your valuables from Sister's office.' She had been told that when they arrived.

'What valuables?' asked Annie.

'Personal belongings,' said Adam. 'Watch, rings, handbag, that sort of thing.'

'And your clothes from your locker,' added Catrin. She looked around and a nurse came to open the locker beside the bed and take out a plastic bag.

'My goodness!' Annie heard her mother say, and she turned her head. She knew she had been cut, a deep gash on her arm had stitches, but if there was blood on her clothes she wished someone else had taken them away.

'It's mud,' said her mother. 'Your dress is covered in mud!'

'Is it?' That must have happened after they lifted her out of the wreck.

'Where was I when the car crashed?' she asked.

'Coming down Chapel Street,' said her mother. 'Your brakes must have failed at the bottom of the hill and you skidded and overturned. The road was slippery, it was raining. Don't you remember?'

'I remember leaving home. Then I don't. What time was it?'

'About five,' said Adam.

She had left just after lunch. 'Where had I been?'

'I don't know,' said her mother.

'Meg's?' Chapel Street was not far from Megan and Barry's.

'She hadn't seen you since Friday,' said her mother.

Annie had no doubt it would all come back to her, but she wouldn't think about it now. She was too confused today for problems.

When Dr Parry did his morning rounds Annie's breathing was bothering her. She was propped up, but every breath hurt, and he didn't have much immediate comfort, because it would go on hurting until the ribs mended. That usually took around four weeks, the physiotherapist would be in later to start her on deep-breathing exercises, everything was under control. He frowned down at the chart but allowed himself a wintry smile when she said, 'I don't think I'd better ask for a mirror, had I?'

'Give it a day or two, you're not a pretty sight.'

'I don't feel pretty,' she said glumly. 'And I don't seem to be able to remember much before the accident.'

'How long before?'

'Two to three hours. Will it come back?'

'Probably. It's quite usual. Don't let it worry you.'

Annie was feeling so groggy it was no wonder she couldn't think straight, and when the doctor moved across to another of his patients she tried to remember. She hadn't bothered before. The morning's tests and treatments had been exhausting enough without taxing her stupefied mind, but now she tried to concentrate on what *had* happened to her before the accident.

She was clear enough why she had gone out. It was because Mrs Lloyd Williams was coming round, but beyond getting the car out of the drive she couldn't remember a thing until after she had crashed. The memory lapse niggled on the edge of her consciousness, although she was sure that someone would soon fill in the gap for her.

Her mother came during the afternoon visiting hour, bringing a neighbour who had given her a lift. Bronwen Pugh was a well-meaning but tactless little woman—you could always rely on Bronwen to put her foot in it—and when she saw Annie she yelped, 'Oh, but there's nasty! Will it get better? You won't look like this for ever, will you?'

Her voice rose higher with each sentence and Catrin said sharply, 'Of course she'll get better. It's only bruises, the face.'

And Bronwen sat down, absentmindedly eating the grapes she had brought, while Catrin went round to read the signatures on the get-well cards. Practically everyone in the office had sent one. The stationer's shop near the *Bugle* building must have done a brisk trade. Annie thought Megan had probably bought a job lot and then bullied everybody to pay up and write a line for Annie.

'All your boy-friends, are they?' enquired Bronwen. 'I often say to my Bill, "There's Annie with another." Well,' as Catrin looked pained, 'Annie's the prettiest girl for miles, we all know that, and we hope she's going to be again, don't we, although I must say she has made a shocking mess of her face.'

Annie had to cough then and it made her wince and hunch over. 'They say ribs mend themselves,' she gasped, 'only it takes time.'

'Well, you only broke them on Sunday,' Bronwen pointed out, and that reminded Annie to ask her mother,

'Did anyone tell you where I was on Sunday? I still can't remember.'

Nobody had, and Bronwen was intrigued. 'Can't you remember anything?'

'Not for a few hours,' said Annie. 'It's probably this bump on my head.'

'Ooh,' Bronwen made a little joke, 'you could have been up to anything!' and Annie gave a weak smile while Catrin asked, 'Is there a card from Adam?'

'The little white one that came with the flowers, by the red rose.'

'I do love a red rose.' Catrin leaned over the single-stemmed vase and sniffed. 'Beautiful scent.' She read the card, 'From one crock to another,' and looked blank for a moment, then smiled. 'He's such a strong masterful man that you forget, don't you, that he was out of action himself not so long ago?'

Annie could have told them that Adam's scars were still healing, and it could be because he remembered how it felt to be lying helpless and hurt that he was being so kind to her.

Megan, and Miss Grey, Adam's secretary, came visiting in the evening. They looked at the get-well cards too and admired the flowers and read Adam's message. 'From the boss?' asked Megan. 'Did he sent you a rose?'

'He sent most of the flowers,' said Annie.

'Your mother,' Megan began, 'thinks——'

'You know my mother,' said Annie. 'She's a great romancer.'

'I wouldn't mind being in here, if it meant Mr Corbett was going to send me flowers,' Miss Grey said wistfully. 'Oh, he is a lovely man!'

'Talk of the devil,' Megan grinned, and Miss Grey's matronly face blushed a girlish pink because Adam had just come into the ward. 'We'd better be going,' said Megan. 'I'll tell them all you sent your love. It's not nearly as much fun at the office without you, we don't get half the laughs.'

She and Miss Grey stopped to exchange a few words with Adam and then he came towards the bed, and Annie was so glad to see him. She was feeling sorry for herself, she needed the comfort of pretending he wouldn't miss a day because he was worried to death about her.

'Hello,' she said.

'Hello.' He drew up a chair and sat close beside her. 'I want to talk to you,' and he looked so serious that she was terrified.

'It isn't about my father?'

'Your father's fine. How are you?'

'Mending, I suppose.' Did he think she might not be? 'I am going to be all right?'

'Of course you are. We'll have you home for the weekend.'

He said 'we' as if she was going home to him and she could dream around that, but he looked grim and she asked, 'So what is it?'

'Have you remembered where you were before the accident?'

'No.' Her mouth was suddenly dry. 'Do you know?'

'There was mud on your dress and your hands as if you'd fallen,' he explained. 'But there's no mud where the car crashed. Your father says you always wear a seat-belt, so it looks as if you drove away from somewhere in a hurry, after you fell in the mud.'

It brought back no memories, no pictures came into

her mind, and Annie said, 'I don't *know*, I can't *remember*.' Visitors round one of the beds burst out laughing. There were a lot of visitors tonight, every patient seemed to have them, all chattering away, and the noise was making her head ache.

'Try,' said Adam. 'I want to know if Jud Dane had any part in this.'

Jud Dane's man had threatened her, but she couldn't believe that Jud would be stupid enough to risk an actual physical attack. Where would that get him? And she didn't want Adam or the *Bugle* getting involved, because accusations like that could end in big legal trouble. She said, 'I could just have slipped down before I got into the car.'

'You could,' he agreed, 'but I want to know as soon as you remember anything,' and she wondered if this was concern for her or whether the reporter in him had to get the record straight. His eyes seemed hard, boring into her poor fuddled brain, and he had a mind as sharp as a scalpel and she wanted him to stop questioning her.

She said bitterly, 'You'll be the first, but I warn you, I don't think there's a story in it.' More shrieks of merriment came from the bed in the far corner and the throbbing in her head was excruciating. 'I think someone smuggled a hyena in with the visitors,' she said. 'I'm not up to an interrogation,' and she closed her eyes and kept them closed until she heard him move away.

She was feeling ragged, and next day was not much better. Adam phoned at midday and they brought the phone to her. 'How are you?' he asked, and she tried to give a light laugh that didn't come off.

'I'd feel easier if I didn't have to breathe. It's like little knives!'

'I know,' he said, and he probably did. He talked to her for a few minutes, giving her office news, and said he would be along later, bringing her mother to see her.

'Nurse says we're not to get you excited,' said her mother that evening, and Annie had to smile, although she was due for depression to strike. She was physically and mentally battered, and her antibiotic intake had been increased to fight the chest infection. She lay there, in pain and in a state of dull misery, listening to her mother's soft lilting voice reading a long dull letter that had arrived at home this morning from one of her mother's friends, until Adam said, 'I think we should be going.'

Annie gave a little nod and Catrin said, 'You do?' and got up and hovered over the bed, wondering where she could plant a kiss between the bruises. Her lips trembled and her eyes filled with tears. 'Get better, my baby,' she whispered as she turned away.

Adam looked down and asked, 'Tired?'

'Yes.' He didn't move, he just went on looking at her, and Annie muttered, 'The doctor says it will be months before I'm right. Months seems an awfully long time,' and she had so little strength.

'Don't think about that,' he said, 'think about home on Saturday.' He made her feel that she could draw strength from him, that if he put his hands on her life would flow into her, although she knew that she mustn't read anything into this but kindness, she must not let herself become dependent on him. 'Promises, promises,' she said, and he smiled and stooped to kiss her cheek, very gently.

'Trust me,' he said, and she said, 'Sure,' and it came out quite gaily and she smiled too.

Next day they had the infection under control and Annie was starting her recovery. At least eight weeks, Dr Parry had said, before she could hope to return to work, but she had Saturday as her probable date of discharge from hospital, and on Friday afternoon when Charlie looked in she was sitting up in bed, her hair freshly washed and fluffy.

She was still a sorry sight. Yesterday was the first time she had dared look into a mirror and she had been horrified, but the swelling was going down, although it was still a reflection she hardly recognised.

It was her facial injuries that struck visitors first, of course, but nobody was as shaken as Charlie, not even Bronwen. He came jauntily into the ward, flirting with the nurses, until he saw Annie. From his expression when he set eyes on her she could have been a monster from outer space. His lips framed, 'My God!' and he couldn't get out another word.

'Sit down,' said Annie solicitously. 'Do you want a glass of water?' Charlie slumped on to a chair, and Annie didn't laugh. If there had been any risk of permanent disfigurement his reaction could have destroyed her, but there was not, and that made it funny. Some sickbed visitor he was, croaking, 'I didn't know you.'

She deliberately misunderstood. 'They'll take the plaster off in about six weeks.'

'Not your arm—your face.'

'It was a joke, I know you meant my face. But my face will be all right—you should have seen me on Monday!' Charlie shuddered and she added, 'On second thoughts, you shouldn't.'

He took out a handkerchief and mopped his brow. 'Any funny stories?' asked Annie, 'I could use a laugh.'

Charlie made an effort. He was thinking of changing his car and he told her about a couple he'd seen, which was hardly riveting entertainment. He said that Adam still had everybody on the hop at the office and was stirring things at the Town Hall, and altogether life was a lot livelier than it had been in Rocky's day. Then he gave her another look and broke off to ask, 'Is your nose broken?'

'No, it's just puffy. Nothing got broken above my ribcage.'

She supposed Charlie was imagining her coming out of this with a boxer's flattened nose. She had always taken prettiness for granted, there had never been a time when she had not been a stunner, but she knew now what it would be like to be ugly. Not many people could see beneath the skin, not many bothered to try. She said, 'By the time I come back to work I'll be quite presentable.'

'I'm certainly glad to hear that.' He could see now that it was just bruising and swelling. No cuts, and her teeth were still straight and perfect.

'I'm going home tomorrow,' she told him. 'Come round in a fortnight and I'll have a better face to show you.'

She had another visitor that day who did nothing for her morale. Mrs Lloyd Williams, in a pink suit, with a pink hat on her pink hair and carrying a clashing bunch of purple asters, arrived on Friday evening. When the visitors were admitted to the ward she was the only one for Annie, and that was lousy luck. Most visiting hours Annie had had friends arriving, but she was going home in the morning, so it looked as if no one else was coming tonight who might have protected her from David's mother.

No way had Germaine Lloyd Williams come from kindness. She said the usual things, 'Hello, how are you? Feeling better, are you?' But her smile and her eyes gloated when she sat down and took a good look at Annie.

Then she put the flowers on top of the locker, flattening the get-well cards, and said, 'You did make a mess of yourself. I don't suppose your face will ever be the same again.'

Annie almost said, 'Hard luck, but it's going to get better. You should have brought a camera and taken a picture, then you could remember me like this.' But she still lacked the strength to be aggressive, so she sighed and lay still and let David's mother tell her how sorry she was about Douglas Bennett's latest heart attack, sighing at all the grief Annie had caused him.

It was true, but it was a cruel thing to say. Annie was already blaming herself, although the accident had been an accident, and when Adam walked into the ward she had never been more glad to see him.

'Adam!' she cried, struggling to sit up, and Mrs Lloyd Williams said,

'I wonder you're letting your men friends see you like this. You're not a pretty face any more, are you?'

She went past Adam with a tight-lipped smile. She had recognised him, but he didn't know her, and as he reached Annie's bed he asked, 'What was amusing the pink lady?'

'Seeing me getting my come-uppance,' said Annie.

'Very charitable. Who is she?'

'She would have been my mother-in-law.'

'No wonder you ran!' Her smile lit from his, and she took one of the deep breaths they kept urging her to take, painful but healing. With Adam here she could smile and breathe.

'Charlie looked in this afternoon,' she told him, 'and nearly fainted when he saw me. I think he was scared he might have to go out on stories with somebody looking punchy. I never suspected he was so sensitive.'

'Neither did I,' said Adam. 'I thought he was just thick.'

Annie giggled, 'Well, that as well,' but there was not much to laugh at. She was battered and bruised and broken and the future was bleak.

'How's my father?' she asked, and before Adam could speak, 'I'm worried sick about him and he's going to worry himself to death about me. I mean, look at me, I'm about as much use as a babe in arms. They're both going to start rushing around, getting themselves worked up, and with his heart——' she sighed despairingly. 'What *am* I going to do?'

She didn't expect an answer, but she got one. 'We might tell them you're marrying me,' said Adam.

CHAPTER SEVEN

ANNIE knew what she had heard, but she couldn't believe she had heard it. Her lips twitched—more in a nervous tic than a smile—and she said very slowly. 'That is a thought.'

'So think about it,' said Adam.

'You're joking.'

'No. If I'm responsible for you it might stop them worrying until you're fit again, and then you could have a change of heart.'

Well, of course she hadn't imagined it was a real proposal, but if there seemed to be an understanding between her and Adam it would take the strain from her parents. Later, when she was stronger, it could peter out, but now it would be lovely to have him to lean on. 'What about Eunice?' she asked.

'She'll understand.' Eunice wasn't that understanding, Eunice would probably blow it, but Annie would have to risk that. She hesitated, although she wanted to shout, '*Yes*!'

'It would make things easier for me, of course,' she said, 'but ever since you came you've had a basinful with my family, one way and another. Are you sure?'

'Sure that I like your family. Your father was on the D-Day beaches with mine, he's a brave man, and now he's under more strain than his heart should be taking. Last Sunday did him no good, and you're still not a reassuring sight.' He smiled. 'Well, put it this way, you don't look up to fighting your own battles yet.'

It would be battle enough getting well. She would try to be cheerful when she got home tomorrow, but broken bones and bruised skin sapped your stamina, and Adam could be such a support.

'I'm not,' she said. 'Yes, please, I wish you would tell them they don't need to worry about me. When things are back to normal we'll have second thoughts, of course.'

'Of course.'

He stayed with her until visiting hour ended, talking, making her laugh softly. Annie didn't know how long it would be before she was able to laugh out loud again. Little muted giggles were all she could manage yet, but he kept her smiling, describing his day.

The nurse picked up the asters and stuck them into one of the not-quite-full vases and stopped to make eyes at Adam. When he had gone she said, only half joking, 'We'll be sorry to be losing you tomorrow, especially as we won't be seeing him any more,' and Annie wondered if she should say, 'He's asked me to marry him,' just to get the feel of it.

In a way he had. Her friends and workmates knew that Adam Corbett lodged with the Bennetts, and that he had been here each day visiting Annie; but nobody would be expecting to hear that he had asked her to marry him.

Perhaps, to be fair, she should tell Megan the reasons, or on the other hand it might be better if she let Adam handle it, saying what he wanted to say. She would play it as it came, never forgetting that it was all pretence. But it made her feel so much happier and stronger, because it meant that he was really fond of her, and she hugged that knowledge to her heart.

Next morning Megan and her mother came to fetch her. Megan pushed the wheelchair down to the car, although Annie protested that there was nothing wrong with her legs. She had walked around the ward, but her knees had a tendency to buckle, and sitting in the back of the car, well padded with cushions, she wished she had taken the painkillers they had offered her. Although Megan was a careful driver it was an uncomfortable journey.

'Your father's waiting for you,' her mother said. 'It's going to be lovely having you home again.' Catrin didn't say much more, but Megan chattered cheerfully and Annie sat in the back sweating with pain. As they approached the house her mother said suddenly, 'Your father's going to be upset when he sees you.'

Douglas Bennett came out of the front door of the house as Megan turned the car into the drive. Adam was with him, and Catrin scrambled out of the front passenger seat and said, 'I'll just have a word with him and tell him you'll feel better after you've rested, that you're bound to be feeling poorly now.'

Adam opened the back door of the car as Megan came round, and Annie edged herself out and managed a grin. 'My knees are giving,' she said.

'Not them as well,' teased Adam. 'Knees were definitely not on the list.' He steadied her, and she asked,

'Where's your stick?'

'I'm trying to give it up. One crock in the family is enough.' She wanted to say, 'Just keep holding me and I'll make it,' as she walked with him the few steps to the house. Megan stayed where she was, looking puzzled, and Annie knew she was trying to work out what Adam had just said.

Of course Douglas Bennett was shocked to see his daughter. She was hurt, injured, and that hurt him, but her eyes were bright in her bruised face and Adam had his arm around her. Douglas said heartily, 'Well, you went to a lot of trouble to get out of having tea with Germaine.'

'Didn't work either,' said Annie. 'She tracked me down to the hospital and brought me some deadly nightshade.' She walked down the hall between the two men, leaving Catrin gasping with relief, joking with Megan,

'Well, that went a lot better than I expected. Do you

think her father's been at the whisky for Dutch courage?'

'Why not?' said Megan. 'I'll phone in the morning, anything I can do.' Catrin thanked her and Megan drove away, still wondering why Adam Corbett had spoken of himself as family.

Annie was seated on the sofa in the lounge with cushions around her. Her father was at the drinks cabinet and her mother was fussing with a box of medications, and Annie indicated her father with a sidewards glance. 'Yes,' said Adam.

'Thank you,' her lips framed, and her mother said gaily to her father,

'Don't tell me you haven't had a glass already!'

'We waited,' said Douglas, 'although this should be champagne.'

'It should indeed.' Catrin went over to smooth the cushions behind Annie. 'She's home.' But that wasn't what Douglas was celebrating.

'Haven't you told her?' he asked Annie, and couldn't resist breaking the news to Catrin himself. 'Well, I've got some excitement for you, then. Adam's just told me he's asked Annie to marry him!'

Her mother's prayers were being answered, Annie thought wryly, as Catrin dropped the box and hurried across the room and fell on Adam's neck, taking Annie's acceptance for granted. After a few moments of almost hysterical joy she tried to contain her delight, although she was still bubbling with it. 'Well, this *is* a surprise, and when did this happen? Last night? And you never said a word this morning, you naughty girl!' She wagged a finger at Annie. 'But of course, Megan was with us, wasn't she? And of course this is better. Just us.'

She smiled at them all, her smile lingering on her husband. 'Oh, we really should have champagne! Shall we go and see if we can get a bottle?' There was a small off-licence a few minutes away where the call for champagne was limited, but Douglas agreed, and off he and Catrin went, looking carefree and happy.

As the front door closed behind them Annie said, tritely, 'That's made their day.' They would have been content if she had chosen any of the eligible men who would have married her, but Adam Corbett was the son-in-law of their dreams. 'They think their troubles are over,' she said, 'now they've delivered me into safe hands.' She must be getting better, because she couldn't stop talking. 'Mind you, there's those who'll say that your troubles are just starting.'

'Like the lady who brought the deadly nightshade?' said Adam. 'Why did you call the wedding off?'

'I hadn't thought about it hard enough before I said all right. In fact I don't believe I ever did say all right, I just found myself wearing a ring.'

'What made you start thinking?'

Her mother and father imagined they would be holding hands and kissing at least, that even in her battered state she and Adam would be getting together somehow, during the ten minutes or so they were out searching for champagne. Instead here they were, chatting about old times.

'Panic, as the day drew near and I realised I couldn't promise any of the things I should have to promise.'

'And Mrs Lloyd Williams is still bearing malice?'

'Very much. There was an awful fuss, of course, everybody was mad at me at the time. But David met someone else who wasn't local and went to live in Edinburgh. He'd been in his father's firm, so I suppose she blames me for that. But she said she'd never forgive me, and she hasn't. Not in all these years. She really got quite a kick out of my accident. I think she's been wanting to push my face in for years.'

'Talking of the accident,' said Adam, 'You still don't remember what happened.'

'I told you I'd tell you. No, I don't. I can remember what must have been just after, though. Did you have a time when you thought you were dying?'

'Long enough to decide I didn't want to go,' he said.

'Me too. What did you think about?' Annie had only thought with desperate anguish that she might never see him again, but she couldn't tell him that. He wasn't sharing his thoughts, but he smiled, 'As Dr Johnson almost said—when you think it's the end it concentrates the mind wonderfully.'

'Doesn't it just?' She was glad she was home, and all she had to do was get well because Adam would deal with the other problems. She lay back on her pillow and looked at him, and although most of her was aching already, the ache for him stirred deep inside her. She asked, 'Are you sure about this? I mean, I know you're busy and it's going to be a nuisance, just to keep my parents happy. I mean, they're not really your responsibility.'

She knew he wouldn't back out, but when he said, 'I feel some responsibility for you,' she blinked. 'If you can't remember what happened then there's a chance that the article on Jud Dane might have put you in jeopardy, and I put you on to that, so perhaps I owe you some protection. If it's only peace of mind about your father and holding off Mrs Lloyd Williams.'

'I'm sure it wasn't——' she began. Then she stopped, because she did need a protector, and Adam was the one she wanted. She said, 'Well, thank you. Call on me if there's anything I can do for you when I'm on my feet again.'

She lay quietly for a few minutes after that until she heard the front door open and her mother called, 'Cooee, we're back!' and Adam moved his chair nearer the sofa and took her unplastered hand between his. They were taking their time in the hall, and Annie began to smile. 'I'm practically a stretcher case, how do they imagine we're carrying on?'

'Very carefully,' said Adam, and she blushed at the thought of caring and infinitely tender lovemaking easing and healing her.

'We've got something,' said her mother outside the door, and both her father and mother came into the room, Douglas carrying two bottles wrapped in blue tissue paper. 'You're looking better already,' he told Annie, and her mother teased with dancing eyes, 'I always did say love was the best medicine!'

Adam loosed Annie's hand, she wished he hadn't, and she wished the fuss of her parents' first ecstatic surprise and delight was over. When they calmed down she would be able to relax, to rest and recuperate, but now her father went off to find a cloth to hold the bottle while he took out the cork, and her mother went for the champagne glasses, and Annie said drily, 'They couldn't be more relieved if I was nine months pregnant and you were making an honest woman of me! It's crazy, the way they've never believed I could fend for myself. They think I'm so fragile.'

He raised an ironic eyebrow at her lying there. 'They're not far wrong at the moment, and I hate to remind you you're on antibiotics.'

Catrin returned, carrying a tray with four old-fashioned saucer-shaped champagne glasses. 'These were Annie's great-grandmother's,' she informed Adam, 'And I know they don't hold the bubbles in, but who wants to leave champagne in the glass anyway? We'll drink it up before the bubbles can escape.'

'To be honest,' said Douglas, 'they had no champagne, but this is quite a palatable sparkling white.' The cork came out with a reasonable pop and the wine fizzed over, and Annie said,

'I'd better not. I am on these pills.'

Her mother clapped both hands over her mouth, 'But

of *course!*—what are we thinking of? And I'm supposed to be the nurse.'

Catrin was a first-class nurse. She had ministered to an ailing father for years, she cosseted her husband now, and she was going to take such care of Annie; but hearing that Annie and Adam were planning to marry had been almost like having Annie miraculously cured. 'Just a sip, then,' said Catrin, 'and I then want you in bed for a while.'

Annie took her glass and her father made a little speech saying how happy he was and what a grand pair they would make, and Annie couldn't look at Adam. The champagne was not the only thing that was not the genuine article, this was not love they were toasting. It was friendship; and gratitude on Annie's side, and then she looked across and their eyes met and she smiled then.

The phone rang and Catrin nearly dropped her glass in her eagerness to answer it. Annie knew she couldn't wait to tell whoever was calling what was happening here, so that most of Llanaven would soon be hearing that the famous Adam Corbett had fallen for Annie Bennett.

But perhaps Adam didn't want it broadcast. He had said, 'We might tell your parents you're marrying me,' he hadn't said, broadcast it to the whole town. She called, 'Don't say anything yet,' and her mother turned, looking disappointed.

'No? Oh, all right.' She left the door open and kept the call brief, saying that Annie was home and she, Catrin, was busy, and anytime next week would be all right to come round. 'That was Susan,' she reported. 'A school friend,' Annie told Adam. She had just asked him, 'Do you mind us telling people?' and he had said, 'Not at all.'

'Why didn't you want me to tell Susan?' her mother demanded, and Annie said, 'Oh—er—I want to tell Megan first. She might be hurt if I didn't. She's always shared her secrets with me.'

'What secrets?' Catrin laughed a little. 'Megan's life is an open book.'

'Maybe,' said Annie. So were most of the lives of the folk she knew, but Adam was as hard to read as a locked-up library. And she was pretending now that one day he would promise, 'With my body I thee worship' to share body and mind so long as they both should live.

She rested most of the day. She walked around the house a little and did her breathing exercises and took her pills. Getting ready for the night was a lengthy business. Her mother sponged her down, sighing at the sight of her bruises, bathing the laceration on her left arm, putting her into a clean cool cotton nightdress that Catrin had cut open so that it could be slipped on easily, fastening with press studs.

Adam had been out since before lunch, returning early evening. He had come upstairs, bringing a portable television that would be useful when she felt less weary. When she was stronger she wouldn't be able to see enough of him, because the accident hadn't shaken that nonsense out of her. She was still overwhelmingly attracted to him, but tonight it was more restful to have her mother, sitting by her bed, doing some crocheting and talking.

Catrin was deeply content. She had been hoping for this from that first evening that Douglas brought Adam home. She had done her best to help, turning her studio into a bedsitter and getting him here, but it was lovely to hear that Adam did want to marry Annie and take care of her.

'I knew all along,' said Catrin happily, 'that he was so right for you, you've always needed a strong man. Have you decided when you might be getting married?'

'No,' Annie said sharply, because she had to stop that right away or her mother would be making out guest lists and planning a reception. 'This isn't a mad passionate affair. We've got all the time in the world, and I like the idea of being engaged, and there's absolutely no rush at all.'

'Very sensible,' said Catrin, who could hardly have said anything else after her own years of waiting. But Annie thought, if Adam asked me I would go to him anywhere. I wouldn't waste a minute longer than it would take me to fall into his arms.

'Were you surprised when he proposed?' Catrin wanted to know.

'It was the biggest surprise of my life,' said Annie.

'I was surprised,' Catrin admitted. She was working on a traycloth for the Mothers' Union Sale of Work, and now she would begin getting little things together again for Annie's bottom drawer. She sat with her head bowed over her work as she talked. 'You know, sometimes your father and I have worried about you, and it's no use saying you don't need somebody looking after you, especially after this.' She pulled the hook through, looping the cotton thread, surveying it with a little frown. 'I was sorry you broke up with Huw,' she said. 'He's probably going to be upset when he hears you're engaged to Adam. Poor Huw! But of course Adam will be much better for you. And the accident seems to have made him realise how much you mean to him, so even that seems to be turning out for the best.'

Annie lay still and her mother sat for a while, doing her crocheting, letting Annie sleep, she thought. Only Annie was not sleeping, and she would ask for a sleeping pill before her mother went to bed or she would be lying awake.

The memory of before the car crash would have surfaced before if she had let herself think about it, because it had been an accident and it had been her fault.

She had been so angry when she saw Huw get out of that car. She was wretched enough as it was, thinking of Adam with Eunice. She hadn't dared stay at home that afternoon because a few well chosen barbs from Mrs Lloyd Williams could have had her screaming, and now Huw! She would almost have preferred Germaine.

'Are you following me?' she had demanded as he came towards her. 'Have you been spying on me?' and he didn't deny it, in fact he sounded quite triumphant.

'I saw you last night, if that's what you mean. I know where you spend your nights. That's why you threw me over, isn't it? Because you'd got your eye on a bigger fish.'

She was not standing for him shadowing her, it gave her the shivers. Anyhow, she hadn't met Adam when she finished with Huw, but Huw preferred to blame a rival.

He had been keeping a watch on her to prove it, and much good would it do him.

'Well, you've picked the wrong one this time,' he told her, and he'd grinned, so that his cheeks plumped out and his eyes went small and he looked like a fat cat with the cream. 'You're out of your league this time, beauty, you won't be much more than a one-night stand with him.' He went on grinning until she said savagely,

'If you've been skulking in the bushes, and you can count, you'll know it's been longer than a one-night stand already, and it's more than likely that it's going to last, because it's very good, and Adam thinks so too.'

He called her a cheap little two-timing tramp, and she raised an arm to hit him, swinging wildly and missing and going sprawling in the mud. He gave a great guffaw of laughter, then got into his car and drove away, while Annie sat there. She had banged her head against her car door and now it was as though she was in a belfry with a migraine and all the bells pealing. She couldn't go home like this, not until she had washed and pulled herself together, and she thought, Megan—I'll go to Megan's.

She slumped behind the wheel of her car, driving it on to the rough track, bouncing down the hill, and she was only five minutes away when she tasted bile in her mouth, and gagged and lost control briefly and tried to pull on the brakes as she went into a skid . . .

She would have to tell Adam. Huw had been out to row with her, she supposed, or maybe make her admit there was nothing lasting between her and Adam. But she had lied because she was angry, saying she was sleeping with Adam and it was marvellous, and she had nearly knocked herself out trying to thump him.

She wasn't going to get much sympathy from Adam over this. 'Is Adam downstairs?' she asked her mother.

'He was talking to your father. Do you want me to see?'

'I'd like to talk to him,' said Annie.

'He may have gone over to the studio.' It was nearly half past ten now. Catrin had been up here all evening and was thinking of going down and making the hot milk drinks for Douglas and herself when Annie opened her eyes and asked for Adam.

'Please get him,' said Annie, and her mother asked anxiously, 'How are you feeling?'

'It isn't a relapse, I'd just sleep better.'

'I'll fetch him,' said Catrin.

He must have been in the loft, because it was several minutes before he came into the room, alone, closing the door behind him. Annie's bedroom was a sunshine room, with yellow mimosa-patterned wallpaper and curtains and duvet. Every few years it was redecorated, usually with new curtains and bedspread, but it never really changed except in colour. There was no chair that Adam could sit on in comfort. The little white wicker armchair and the satin-topped dressing table stool were fragile feminine things. He was a big man in every way, so tall that he made the room seem even smaller.

It wasn't going to be easy admitting how she had blown her top with Huw Sanders. She had had some provocation, he shouldn't have been following her, but it was a silly tale and it meant that she had slapped him first. Adam need not blame himself for her car crash, because the Jud Dane story had had nothing to do with it.

She stammered, 'I want to talk to you, but my eyes are getting tired, so would you please turn out a few lights?'

As well as the overhead light there was a small fat yellow lamp burning on top of the chest of drawers. He switched off the main light, but the room was still too bright, confessionals should be dark, and Annie croaked, 'That one too, please.'

It wasn't a terrible confession, just a stupid one, proving that she could be so silly that Adam would probably despair of her. He sat on the side of the bed and she could see his face quite clearly, although it was dark and she had her eyes closed. She said, 'Did you mind me asking you to come up here? Were you working?'

'How do you feel?' She could feel him leaning towards her.

'I ache,' she said.

'Poor Annie!' She thought he could have said 'poor kitten' in much the same way if he had opened a door on a half-drowned cat and let it in from the storm, and she asked wistfully, 'Was it a shock to you when you heard that I'd crashed?'

'A hell of a shock.'

She was sure the news hadn't thrown him off course at all. He was a man who would always cope, and she wondered if anything in the world could make him crack up. 'Would you have missed me,' she asked, 'if I hadn't come round?'

'I would have missed you.' Perhaps he would, although he was humouring her. 'The gaiety would have gone out of the *Bugle* for a start.'

'Megan said they weren't having so many laughs without me.'

There would be some flabbergasted faces at work on

Monday when they heard that Adam Corbett was supposed to be marrying Annie Bennett, and she asked, 'Do you think they'll swallow this tale?'

'Why not?'

'Well, most of them are journalists, they ought to be able to tell fact from fiction. But I suppose it doesn't matter much so long as my father believes it and it keeps him happy, and he gets his strength back and I get mine. He is happy, isn't he?'

'I think so. He's been asking about my prospects.' Adam chuckled and Annie gasped, 'He *hasn't*? Oh, lor', how embarrassing! I do apologise.'

'I found it rather touching. He's one of the old school when fathers of daughters were expected to do that. I think I managed to reassure him, and he's prepared to overlook me being out of the country from time to time because much of the time that's where the news is, and he'd prefer me at the top of my profession.'

Her father knew Adam's status, and he would have enjoyed discussing it because he was thrilled to bits that Annie had apparently acquired such a successful man. Luckily Adam didn't mind, but she groaned, 'Anything else he wanted to know?'

'Where I would be taking you to live.'

This was just talk, because Adam would be taking Annie nowhere, and she sighed so deeply that her cracked ribs hurt, making her clench her teeth as he went on, 'I told him that I have a London flat and a villa in Rhodes. The villa interests him. It seems your parents went to Rhodes on their honeymoon.'

'Yes, they did.'

'Well, they're going again as soon as his doctor gives him the all clear, and he thinks it would be following a romantic tradition if we did.'

'You and me?'

'On our honeymoon.'

'What did you say to that?'

'Nothing.'

'Do you know how long they were engaged?' Annie said shrilly, trying to sound indignant. 'Over ten years. It has to be a record, but they'd better believe that's an old family tradition too. Oh dear,' and she sighed again, but shallowly this time, 'and I thought we could just say we had an understanding and they'd stop worrying about me. I didn't think he'd be asking to see your bank statements.'

'He took my word I was solvent.' But really her father had a nerve, sounding Adam out to see if he could keep Annie in style, when everybody knew that the manner to which she was accustomed was so modest that he could probably have kept half a dozen women in it without feeling the pinch. '*And* he books a holiday in your villa, he *must* be feeling better.'

'It does seem to be working.'

'Can they go there? I mean——?' She meant, was it Eunice's home too, but Adam said, 'Of course. Most of my friends use it.'

Somewhere you could pack up and fly off to any time, it sounded lovely. Right now her body felt as weighed down as if she was encased in plaster instead of just her arm, and the idea of being lightfooted and agile again was like a dream. She said, 'Please tell me about it—how it is when the sun's shining. I don't want to take a sleeping pill, and it's a long time since I had a bedtime story, but I seem to remember they used to work.'

In a few words he had her driving along the winding mountain roads. She could taste the dust and feel the sun on her face; and then the villa, with its white walls and tiled floors, and worn marble steps leading down to blue water under a cloudless sky.

When she really got there, if she ever did, she would be able to run and dance again. And if Adam was there too they could swim and walk together, talk and sit close. Perhaps lie close with his arms around her, in some other room as warm and as dark as this.

This night, a week ago, she had gone across to the loft to lie in Adam's bed, because she couldn't rest in her own; and Huw had been skulking in the shadows, watching the light go out.

She should be telling Adam this and she would, but now she put her head on his shoulder and she knew that tonight she could do nothing that might spoil this rapport. As long as he felt responsible for her it was almost like loving her, and another day or two wouldn't hurt.

She would fall asleep more easily if he stayed here, she didn't want him to leave her. 'Will you sleep now? he asked, and she said, 'I expect so. Well, I can see you can't hang around all night. Good night, thank you,' and running straight on, 'Did you and my father drink all that wine that was passing for champagne?'

'No.'

She was still leaning on him and he had an arm behind her on the pillows. Even the way she was she fitted so comfortably against him. 'I bet you never get drunk,' she said.

'Not for a long time.' His voice was deep, slow, amused and she said, 'I can't remember ever getting so tight as I did that night.'

'Make love to me,' she had said. She must have been right out of her mind if she had thought she had a hope in hell of seducing Adam. She said into the darkness, 'Well, I warned you I had a crush on you. I suppose I thought if you did make love to me I'd get over it, get you out of my system.'

'That's a rare compliment.' He was laughing now. 'You don't credit me with much expertise.'

'Oh, but I do, I do.' She could be outrageous and get away with it while she was still ill. So long as she spoke gaily it would just be a sign that she was not letting her injuries get her down. She said, 'In fact I think it's as well you didn't take up my offer, or my crush would have developed into an obsession, and wouldn't that be awful?'

'Awful,' he agreed, and as he stood up she lifted her face. He hesitated for a moment, then he leaned over and kissed her, and her lips parted softly and urgently against his mouth. Annie wanted to reach up and cling to him, but there was no strength in her hands. It was all she could do to sit up, keeping her head back, although she would not have broken off the kiss first.

When he did she fell back on her pillows, feeling spent. 'I'll leave the door open,' he said. Her mother's door would be open during the night just down the corridor, and she almost said, 'I'd rather you stayed.' But that would be asking too much, so instead she said, 'I'm glad I'm home.'

'I'm glad too,' said Adam.

She smiled; she could do that now without the smile hurting her face. She could manage quite a grin. She smiled again when her mother came in to ask if she wanted a hot drink. No, she said, she didn't think so, and she thought she could get to sleep. Then she lay awake, wondering for how long she would be practically untouchable and how soon she could be handled and held passionately, and how she could make Adam want to love her rather than comfort her . . .

Her father looked in while she was drinking her first cup of tea next morning and asked her if she knew that Adam had a villa in Rhodes.

'I do now,' she said.

'Your mother and I are going over there.' 'Not until Annie's well, of course,' her mother had stressed, and Annie had said, 'Lovely.'

They would look forward to it, it would be a second honeymoon for them. Theirs had been a gentle love story, and they thought now that Annie had found the same kind of relationship, a safe harbour where no storm blew. It never occurred to them that Annie might not want a safe harbour.

She thought they both looked years younger this morning, and she wouldn't think about the time when the masquerade had to end, because Adam had said he was not the marrying kind, and unless he did marry somebody else this could keep her parents happy for years. They knew all about long engagements and he was abroad a lot. They could go on believing he was going to take care of Annie, that she was never going to be lonely.

Now her mother fixed the tray-stand over her knees. Breakfast looked tempting, on a white embroidered cloth: coffee and orange juice and a brown boiled egg, 'soldiers' cut thin and crustless. There was a pink rosebud on a linen napkin and two newspapers neatly folded.

'There's going to be no more dashing off without breakfast for a long time,' Catrin reminded her. 'I'm going to feed you up. You've always been too thin.'

No early morning work-outs either, just breathing exercises, and the effort of getting herself washed and dressed. She was going to be housebound for a week or so, and slowed down for much longer than that. Just now she was too frail to fret, but as she had hardly had a day's illness before the accident she might prove a rotten patient as soon as boredom and frustration set in. Her mother would humour her, but if Adam was around he would stand for no nonsense, which could be as well.

She sipped her orange juice and picked up a newspaper. 'Adam's made a few notes,' said her mother. 'Things he thinks might interest you.' Alongside a headline on a business merger he had written 'Mafia', and under the picture of an actress, who had landed the starring role in a musical spectacular and said she owed it all to her husband's encouragement, '*Whose* husband?' There were several more, and it livened up the papers no end wondering what the cryptic notes meant. One thing was sure, they were mostly libellous.

As she turned the pages her mother, who had no idea what kind of dynamite this was, said, 'It's nice you both being journalists. You'll be able to travel together, won't you? Not the dangerous places, of course, but he does go to other places. You'll have a wonderful life.'

'Yes,' said Annie, and for a moment it was as though all that was waiting for her, the togetherness and the danger. 'Wouldn't you miss me?' she asked.

'Of course, but you'd both be coming back. You can always get a plane these days.'

I wonder, thought Annie, if there's any way I could tag along. I wonder if he'd let me. She asked, 'Is Adam downstairs?'

'I'm not letting him up until you've had your breakfast and we've made you look prettier.'

Annie smiled wryly, 'There's not much we can do about that unless I wear a yashmak!'

But she did finish her breakfast, and then her mother had to help her wash, and the plaster cast on her arm meant that she couldn't get into most of her clothes. 'I've got just the thing,' said Catrin, hurrying off and coming back with a Japanese kimono in midnight blue satin, embroidered on the back with scarlet and gold peonies. Annie had bought it for her two Christmases ago and she wore it sometimes in the evenings when she and Douglas gave little dinner parties for friends.

The sleeves were wide and the sash fastened the robe around Annie, and when she looked at herself in the dressing table mirror she had to smile. Because her bruises now had a yellowish tinge and one eye was still slittish and slightly Oriental. 'Will you do my hair up?' she said.

She sat on the stool and Catrin lifted her dark

shining hair, pinning it high, sighing from time to time because Annie was undoubtedly a sight, and then smiling because Adam Corbett was going to take care of her and everything was turning out for the best.

Annie came slowly down the stairs, her mother hovering anxiously at her side. 'We're coming down,' her mother had called, and that had brought Annie's father out of the lounge into the hall, another anxious face. Annie smiled for her father and looked for Adam, then she saw him in the doorway.

'I like it,' he said.

'Suits me, doesn't it?' she said. 'Goes with my eye.'

She lowered herself gingerly on to the sofa and her mother lifted her feet up. And she bit her lip until her parents went, leaving her alone with Adam, then she grimaced in a silent scream. 'Is it bad?' he asked. 'Maybe you should take some painkillers.'

'It's better. Eight weeks, they said, and this is only the first, but I've never been ill before.'

'It does come as a shock,' he agreed.

It was forging a link between them where there was no real link before, and she said, 'I can't wait to hear whose husband encouraged Carole Denvers.' He told her the name of a politician and she said, 'You're putting me on.'

'Not a bit of it. He put money into the show, and she is his latest.'

'His *latest*?'

'That's right. He fancies himself as a free-ranger. Fortunately so does his wife, her range is every bit as extensive as his.'

'Goodness,' said Annie. 'And what about the Mafia, then?'

She wondered if Adam was making it up, because it was all very surprising. It had her goggling and gasping, and it certainly took her mind off her aches and pains.

There was a fire burning, the weather had cooled

dramatically since last weekend, and when they had gone through the two newspapers he screwed up the pages on which he had written notes and held them down with the poker until they were ashes. Annie was suddenly sure then that it was all true. 'You don't half know a lot, don't you?' she said.

'A tool of the trade.' He smiled across at her from the fireplace. 'A filing cabinet in your head. What you see and hear you remember. Most of it you keep to yourself, but occasionally it can be useful.'

In dealing with the likes of Jud Dane, she thought, and she should be telling him about Huw, and she would when she was stronger. The phone had rung a couple of times while they were talking. It rang again now, and this time her mother looked in and asked, 'Do you want to speak to Megan?'

'How are you?' asked Megan as Annie picked up the phone.

'Not too bad.'

'Good. Is Adam still there?'

He had come into the hall with Annie and gone through the back door into the garden to walk across to his own room. She had watched him go before she picked up the phone in her left hand. Now she said, 'I've got something to tell you. We could be getting married some time.'

There was three seconds' silence, then Megan screeched, 'You and Adam Corbett? You're fooling!'

'I'm not.'

'I can't believe it. I mean—*him*! I mean, how do you do it? How do you *do* it? What about Eunice Fleming?'

Annie could hardly explain here, while her mother and father were around, and Megan rattled on, 'She's in Acapulco, isn't she? I read that she was off to do some research for a book. Well, they can't have been as close as we thought, can they? Was it the accident? You said there was nothing, didn't you? Did the accident change things?'

'Yes,' said Annie, and it had.

'Barry ...' she heard Megan yelling—between Megan and her mother the news would be all over town in no time—and then Megan spoke into the phone again. 'I'm thrilled for you, I really am.' Another briefer pause. 'At least I think I am, but you're taking something on. I mean, he's outstanding.' She sounded none too sure that Annie could live up to Adam's brilliance. 'Oh, I do hope it all works out!'

'So do I,' said Annie fervently, and she heard Megan telling Barry,

'You'll never guess——' and she put down the receiver. At her side her mother asked, 'Well, now can I tell our friends?' and without waiting for Annie's reply Catrin picked up the phone and began to dial.

For most of the morning when Catrin was not on the phone it seemed to be ringing. Annie closed her ears to it, and sat in an armchair with the rest of the Sunday papers. Her mother was full of energy today, her spirits as buoyant as though she was a bride-to-be herself; and her father was relaxed and smiling, and Annie knew how much it meant to him, believing he had Adam as a son. And he had, for as long as Annie could swing it. If she played her part, sweetly and undemandingly, Adam might even get used to her being his lady.

During the afternoon she rested on her bed, curtains drawn—her mother had insisted on that. She slept, waking as Catrin drew back the curtains, letting in the cool grey evening light.

'All right?' Her mother smiled as Annie lifted her head. 'You see, you did need rest, you have been to sleep. Although I wonder the phone didn't wake you, there've been a lot of calls.'

She lifted down the kimono that was hanging on a coathanger on the outside of the wardrobe, and with her back to Annie said, 'Huw rang. He spoke to Adam.'

CHAPTER EIGHT

'WHAT does Huw want?' Now it was too late Annie would have given a great deal to have got her version in first.

'I was round at Bronwen's,' said her mother, 'and when I came back your father said Huw had phoned and asked to speak to you and Adam had taken it. He was playing chess with your father, Adam was.' Catrin laid the kimono across the foot of the bed. 'I don't think Huw could have said anything—well, unpleasant. Adam said he was asking how you were.'

She meant that Adam was as self-controlled as ever, but Annie could have told her that if he had been riled it would not have shown unless he meant it to. He would still have come back from the phone, talked normally, and gone on playing chess, not missing a move. But she was sure herself that Huw would have said enough to put Adam in the picture on what had happened before the accident. She couldn't go on now pretending she didn't remember, and why, oh, why hadn't she told him last night? Or this morning?

'Is Adam here now?' she asked.

'Yes, and so are Bronwen and Bill.' Annie groaned and Catrin said placatingly, 'I had to say come round. As soon as I told her you were engaged she wanted to meet Adam—and she wants to see you too, of course.'

Annie could not go down and face them in front of Adam, because after Bronwen had said what a surprise this talk of marriage was, and asked heaven knows how many personal questions, she was quite likely to enquire if Annie had got her memory back. 'I'll come down when Bronwen's gone,' said Annie. 'She does rattle so, and my head feels thick enough now. I'll just sit here and do my breathing exercises.'

She got into the kimono and sat in the little wicker armchair, which supported her quite well; and her mother fussed around, smoothing the bed, then went downstairs to say that Annie was still resting.

In, slow . . . Annie breathed, out, slow . . . count as you go, trying each time to increase your intake of air. It hurt, but she had to keep doing it, she didn't want to get fluid settling in her lungs again. It made her cough and she was hacking, softly and painfully like an old lady, when the door opened a crack and Bronwen's head poked through.

'Why indeed,' said Bronwen brightly, 'and there she is, up and dressed!'

Catrin, just behind, pulled an apologetic face for Annie. 'Bronwen wasn't going without seeing you.'

Bronwen's affection was warm and genuine, and Annie had to smile. And after her shocked reaction last time it was quite comforting to hear her say, 'It's going down,' as though she was referring to a lift rather than the puffiness of Annie's face. She came into the room and circled Annie with increasing satisfaction.

'Yes, oh yes, I can see the difference—oh, I am pleased! I said to my Bill when I came back from hospital on Tuesday, "Well, I don't know," I said, "but I don't much like the looks of Annie." And what's all this about you getting married? And isn't he a smasher?'

'Not yet,' said Annie, and Bronwen leered,

'No—well, you wouldn't be much use to a man like this, would you? But you're a fool if you keep him waiting any longer than you have to. I know I wouldn't.' She nearly jabbed Annie with her elbow, then thought better of it and nudged Catrin and said, 'Show us your ring, then.'

Annie's left hand was curled in her lap, almost

covered by the sleeve of the kimono, and Bronwen hovered expectantly. eyes down. That was another thing; everybody would be expecting Annie to wear a ring. As soon as she could she must get something that looked suitable. It was hard to tell diamond from man-made these days unless you tried cutting glass.

'She hasn't got one yet,' said Catrin. 'But of course Adam will be buying her a ring.'

'That sudden, was it?' said Bronwen. 'There's romantic! My goodness, Annie,' she looked as if she was recalling a national disaster, 'I remember how your mother carried on when you left young David Lloyd Williams waiting at the church.'

'I didn't——' Annie began, although calling off a wedding just days before was almost as bad as leaving him at the church. She bit her lip and let Bronwen ramble on.

'And I'd like to be a fly on the wall when Germaine Lloyd Williams hears about this! She's never forgiven you for deciding you could do better for yourself than her David. And you have,' Bronwen declared triumphantly. 'A lot better.' She winked, and it was true, Annie had been waiting for Adam without knowing it. The only trouble was that he had not been waiting for her.

'I think we'd better go down now,' said Catrin, and downstairs she said, 'Annie's up now, Adam if you'd like to go to her,' and Bronwen asked, 'When is she going to get a ring?'

Annie said, 'Hello,' as Adam walked in. 'Take a seat,' she said. The only seat, apart from the bed and the chair Annie was sitting on, was the dressing table stool. He sat on that, arms folded, long legs stretched and crossed at the ankles, back resting against the dressing table so that he looked relaxed, and she told him, 'I've been doing my breathing exercises. I can only count up to three yet, after that the stabbing starts. What do I aim for? Twenty?'

'Only if you want to burst your lungs,' he said, and she smiled because that was probably a joke, only he wasn't smiling, so she asked,

'What did Huw Sanders say?'

'He sent his congratulations. He said, "She always thought she could get any man, and it looks as though she's right." He said he hoped I could master you because he couldn't.'

Adam would remember. Every word would go into the filing cabinet of his mind. He spoke as if he was reading a memo. 'He said, "And tell her I was sorry to hear she crashed her car and I'm sure she does remember what happened that afternoon".'

'Oh,' said Annie, and the word dropped like a pebble into a deep well.

'So?' said Adam.

'I only remembered last night,' she said, and his reaction was the slightest lift of one eyebrow. He was waiting and she said, 'The Lloyd Williams were coming to tea on Sunday afternoon and I took off because I couldn't face her.' He knew that, but she was starting at the beginning to work up enough impetus to finish.

'I drove up to the caves. I told you how I thought I'd found Merlin's cave when I was a child, right in the heart of the hills—well, I went up there again, and walked around. And when I came out Huw's car was parked under the trees by my car and he started ranting.

'I finished with Huw the day before you started on the *Bugle*, because he was getting possessive and heavy and it was finished—it was over. But it seems he'd been following me more or less ever since, checking up on me. He was sure it had to be another man, he wouldn't believe it could be him. He was in our garden when I went over to the loft and he decided we were having an affair. It might have looked like that, because on Saturday night you weren't there, but he didn't know that, I went over and I—fell asleep and I didn't come out till morning. And I don't know how long he'd hung around, but he followed me on Sunday afternoon and he was waiting when I came out of the caves to tell me he knew I was sleeping around.'

She hadn't looked at Adam. She had looked anywhere but at him, mostly down at her hands, and Adam said, 'He was mistaken—so what happened next?'

'I was mad at him, so I said yes, I was and so what? And he called me a two-timing little tramp and I tried to hit him.'

'*You* hit *him*?'

'I missed. I swung at him and slipped, and went slithering in the mud and banged my head on the car door.'

'And what did he do?'

'He laughed. Then he got in his car and went.'

'It's as well he's got a sense of humour,' said Adam dryly.

'He hasn't, much. He was just pleased I'd made a fool of myself.'

'You certainly did.' He agreed with her emphatically, 'You've got a man who's jealous enough to be keeping tabs on you, who'd like to master you. You're alone on the moors and you tell him his suspicions are right, and then you take a swing at him.'

There was no need to spell out how idiotic she could be, and she said glumly, 'I know. I suppose I should have said I didn't mind a bit being spied on by somebody hanging around in my garden, and apologised for breathing. It was stupid to lose my temper. And this is my fault too, isn't it?' she gestured towards her broken arm with her left hand, 'because I knocked myself silly on the car door and I hadn't got my brakes fixed, and I suppose you never do anything stupid do you?'

'You are joking?' Saddling himself with Annie's problems was a crazy thing to do, and she said dolefully,

'Well, you know now that the accident was nothing to do with Jud Dane, so you don't have to feel responsible for anything.'

He couldn't opt out, not yet. Taking away his support now would be dealing her father a death blow, and she said, 'But I did have a memory black-out until last night, and I would have told you what happened.'

'I believe you,' and he might as well have added, 'But thousands wouldn't,' and she said in a small voice,

'So what do we do?' She felt her lips trembling, her face going woebegone, and he said, 'Cheer up, it can only get better.'

He wasn't angry, even if he did think he had been 'conned'. He didn't seem all that surprised either, that she had acted without stopping to consider the consequences, which meant he thought she was a fool, but she was glad he didn't go on about it. She made herself smile and she tried to cheer up. She said, 'It's got to be getting better, because Bronwen says I'm not nearly as fat-faced as I was on Tuesday. How long have she and Bill been down there?'

'About half an hour.'

'What was Bronwen talking about?'

'You,' said Adam solemnly, 'How often she's said to her Bill, "There's Annie with another".' He gave a passable imitation of Bronwen's Welsh accent, and Annie grinned,

'No wonder my mother came up to wake me! Now with Mrs Lloyd Williams that would be bitchiness, but Bronwen would think she was singing my praises.'

'She's very fond of you,' he said, 'and she wants to know when we're getting a ring.'

It need not bother Adam, nobody was asking him to wear one, but they would all be eyeing Annie's ring finger. 'I thought when I'm able to get out I might get something that will pass,' she said. 'Like the champagne, it won't be real. Like a theatrical prop.'

Evening shadows were gathering thickly outside the window, and the room seemed very small. There were far horizons out there. Eunice Fleming was in Acapulco and some time somebody would say Eunice's name, but Annie didn't think she would be the one, because for the next two months or so she would be dreaming that when Adam left Llanaven the world would open up for her too.

'Megan's here!' her mother called from the bottom of the stairs. 'Can she come up?'

'Why not?' Annie called back.

Adam stood up as they heard Megan on the stairs, and she came into the room with her coppery hair falling loose over her shoulders, and Annie thought, I wish I could run upstairs like that. Megan gave them both an uncertain smile, as though she was still not sure this was not one of Annie's jokes, and she glanced at her left hand. 'I don't have a ring yet,' said Annie.

'Well, talk about a sensation!' Megan was breathless. 'Everybody's so *surprised*!'

'Are they?' said Adam, and he smiled down at Annie and it was as though he had always been at the very centre of her life, a feeling deep and strange and wonderful. 'Don't overtire her,' he said to Megan.

He closed the door behind him, and Megan collapsed on to the stool and said 'Wow!' and clutched her head. 'I'm still trying to take it in. I never dreamt—well, I suppose I wondered if you'd end having an affair, I thought you were keen on him, but as for *marrying*—I never thought he'd ask in a million years.' She went off on another tack. 'You are a deep one, you said there was nothing going on, why didn't you tell me?'

'Sorry,' said Annie. She couldn't admit, 'It's all pretence.' She said, 'The accident hurried things.'

'I can understand that,' said Megan, 'but—were you before?'

'Lovers?' Megan nodded, and Annie heard herself say, 'Yes,' and she felt that it was true.

'Well,' said Megan with a grin, 'this must be frustrating for you. How do you manage, with cracked ribs and both arms out of action?'

'Very carefully,' said Annie, remembering Adam saying that, and Megan's grin widened even more.

'It's some incentive for getting better! I'll bet you make record progress!'

Next day the stitches were taken out of the gash on Annie's left arm. The district nurse had called in the morning, but her mother was sure that unless complications developed she could manage all the nursing that Annie needed. Dr Parry took the stitches out. Her parents were both his patients, he was keeping an eye on Douglas and pleased at his progress.

He congratulated Annie and said how he admired Adam Corbett's writing, and Annie said, 'Thank you,' keeping her eyes averted as the stitches were snipped.

'There we are.' He straightened, and she turned to look at the scarlet seam on her soft smooth skin. She bit her lip as he assured her, and her mother, that in a few months there would be nothing to show. She knew she was lucky, but until now she had hardly had a blemish, and this looked so disfiguring that she felt depressed every time she saw it.

During the afternoon the girl who had given her a lift home from the barbecue came to see her. Christine was an old schoolmate of Annie's, a nice ordinary girl who had married a boy she had known all her life and the only one who had mentioned marriage by the time she was twenty-one. She left a couple of magazines, and when Adam came in from work Annie was in the lounge looking at one of them, which was open at a page on how to put zip into a dowdy bathroom about which she couldn't care less, although she had been staring at it for ages.

She was glad to see him. She tried to stand up, but she would have needed support to get out of the chair, so she sagged back into it and smiled and asked, 'How was it at the *Bugle*?'

'Congratulations all round,' he said. Annie could imagine. Well, they'd have to congratulate him, but what they would be saying behind his back was another matter. She was sure that her colleagues wished her well, but they would all be staggered at the news.

She said, 'I've just had a visitor who always thought I was a raver but thinks this is going it even for me. She kept saying, "But you've only known each other less than a month and you've spent one week of that in hospital." She went to play-school with her husband.'

Adam smiled. 'Were you a raver?'

'Only in a very little way.'

'How's the arm?'

'Stitchless.' Her sleeve covered it, it would be a long time before she would go sleeveless, but winter was coming. She wrinkled her nose. 'But it looks horrid.'

'I've got something for you.' He took a small blue velvet box out of his pocket, and she said, 'You shouldn't have.' But of course she was as thrilled as a child at Christmas when he opened it on a ring, a heart set with shining stones, and explained,

'It's Victorian crystals. I can't find you the crystal cave, so here's a crystal heart.'

'It's beautiful!' And when he slipped it on her third finger it fitted perfectly.

'Your mother provided one of your rings. She's anxious for you to have something to show the neighbours.'

'You are kind,' she smiled.

'Not particularly, it looks worth more than it is. As

long as they don't start expecting a wedding ring to go with it we're all right.'

Annie knew there would be no wedding ring. This was a friendship ring that one day she would wear on her other hand, but it shone like diamonds with all the colours of the rainbow, so that when she lifted her hand and looked into it it was like looking into the crystal cave.

Catrin peeped round the door, smiling, asking, 'And what's this?' as Annie looked up from the ring, and then going breathless with wonder. 'Oh, but isn't it *beautiful*?'

'Isn't it just?' said Annie.

Her mother's eyes were sparkling, and Adam had bought it for Annie and put it on her finger, and she found her own eyes misting with tears because, crazily, she had never been happier.

Well, she had something to show her visitors now. She had a stream of visitors during that first week home. She was getting stronger every day, even if she did still feel fit for nothing, and her mother was strictly limiting visiting times.

'Aren't you *lucky*?' most of the women said, although if it hadn't been for Adam's ring there wouldn't have been much luck in being smashed up in a car crash. The first reaction was always shock, from those who hadn't seen her in hospital—'Oh, *poor* Annie!'—but the ring made her condition less poignant. She had an arm in plaster and a bruised and puffy face, but she had nabbed the most eligible man in town, and that was quite a consolation prize. 'What a surprise,' they all said, and Annie would say, 'It was to me too,' and that was the truth, and it always made her smile.

They wanted to talk about Adam and so did she. She emphasised that there were no wedding plans yet, it was an engagement, an understanding. But she couldn't help looking at her ring and turning her hand so that the colours flashed, and she couldn't help sounding proud of Adam because she was. He was such a super man, and he was her very good friend, and the evenings with him around were the high spot of her day.

Of course he had his own work to do, and that he did in his own room. As soon as Annie was steady enough to get up those tricky steps she would know she was really on the road to recovery, but this first week she dared not risk it; and when she said, 'I'd like to get to the studio some time,' Adam said, 'You're better where you are for now.'

Each evening her mother and father left them alone for a while, and there was always something to talk about. He gave her a run-down on the day's events on the *Bugle*, and that was always interesting and usually funny. He told her about places he had been to, people he had met, in the years he was away from here, but he never mentioned Eunice and neither did Annie.

He kissed her, coming and going, if anyone was around who would expect them to kiss. But it was a light touch, and she wondered, when she was strong enough to try for more, if the miracle might happen and he might kiss her properly, or if he would put her aside with kindly amusement. The way she looked now she couldn't even be flirtatious. She was so used to being physically attractive that she felt her disfigurements almost as keenly as her helplessness.

Her mother was not sparing herself in any way, and Annie spent most of her time downstairs to save Catrin running up and down, and tried not to be a nuisance. So far she had showered, with Catrin doing the spraying and the drying and looking a little puffed when the ablutions were over. The arm in plaster was cumbersome and painful, but Annie could use her left arm now, and on Saturday evening she went along to the bathroom and washed her hair.

Her parents were watching a film on TV, and as

Annie was supposed to be resting—she had had four visitors this afternoon—her mother might leave her alone a little while before coming upstairs again. Plenty of time to take a proper bath, a scented soak, instead of showering and sponging. She didn't want her mother having to heave her in and out, it was too much for Catrin, but now she was here, sitting on the side of the bath, she was sure she could manage.

The bath had handgrips they had had fitted for her father. She was clumsy, but her mother had adapted clothes to accommodate the plaster on her arm and the tenderness of her ribcage, and she unpopped press-studs and slid off bra and pants and stockings. She was living in loose-fitting housecoats and caftans these days. She had taken a caftan off before she washed her hair, and hung it behind the door, and as the water rose in the bath, filling the small room with steam and the scent of flowers and herbs, she was glad the mirror tiles behind the bath were misting, because a full-length reflection of herself was the last thing she fancied facing. She was still mottled with bruises like an old trout.

She stepped gingerly into the water, which was hotter than she expected but all right after she had stood quite still for a few moments. Everything had to be done very deliberately and carefully. She held on to the left hand grip and went down squatting, keeping her back straight and the arm with the plaster out of the water, resting on the side of the bath. She would just soak, but afterwards she would feel fresher, and she wanted to start doing things for herself and every little helped.

She stretched out her legs in slow motion. Even they were bruised, but at least there were no cracked bones there. Annie leaned back against the end of the bath and lifted a leg a little, so that her foot came up from the sea-green water, through the foam, she thought of waves breaking on a beach. She thought of the villa on Rhodes.

Her feet were fine. She might manage to paint her toenails, scarlet perhaps or gold, and then at least some part of her would be pretty.

It was wonderful lying here. Until you knew what it was like to feel heavy as lead you couldn't appreciate the lovely lightness when you were supported by warm scented water, even a mere bathful. It was a pity about the plastered arm, but the rest of her was enjoying this. She lay, luxuriating, a dopey half-smile on her face, until the water began to cool. Normally she would have stretched over and run more hot, but that would be awkward, and she had probably been in long enough.

When she sat up she winced at the pain in her ribs. She must climb out the way she had got in, with extreme wariness. It should have been possible, she only had to reverse her movements, but it was not going to be easy. Getting in she had slid slowly down. She had to haul herself up to get out, and most of the oil seemed to have settled at the bottom of the bath.

She squirmed, gasping, realising that she would have to make a mighty effort, and suddenly slithering so that her head went under and she came up choking, eyes smarting, sick from the wrench on her broken arm. Now the gashed arm was aching too. Soaking had softened the scar and she felt that any strain might burst it open.

She couldn't get out of the wretched bath. She might work the plug loose if she could get her toes round the chain, but it hurt to move and emptying the water wouldn't lift her up. She shouted 'Mother!' and saw that she had knocked the bottle of bath oil into the water. She hadn't bothered to replace the cap and now the liquid was pouring out in a widening emerald pool.

If her mother and father were listening to the television alone they probably wouldn't hear her. They could give her another hour's 'resting' at least. There wouldn't even be a commercial break, the film was on B.B.C. By the time anyone came upstairs she was going to be sitting in a bath of cold oil, and every bruise on her body started to throb.

'Mother!' she shouted again, and the door opened and Adam said, 'Will I do?'

'Yes, oh yes!' She was not far from panicking. 'Could you stir my mother from in front of the television? I need some help to get out of here.'

'That might take a while. They're out.'

'Could you lift me?'

'I should think so.' He took off his jacket and dropped it on the back of the chair. 'You're supposed to be resting, what's the idea of this?'

'I started washing my hair, then I thought I'd take a bath.'

'You're not safe to be left!' As he leaned over to pull out the plug she ducked down instinctively, slithered again, and sent a green wave over him. 'What the hell are you using for water?' He reached for a towel, mopping his dripping face.

'The bath oil fell in.'

It was leaving her high, if not dry, naked and ugly. The last of the water glugged down the pipe and a thick viscous residue of oil coated the bath. She reached for the towel, but Adam said, 'We'll need this for a footing.' He tucked it underneath her as she cowered, trying to shield herself with her arm.

'I look horrible,' she muttered through chattering teeth.

'You look ridiculous.' He smiled at her. 'And we're both going to look pretty silly if I have to call Bronwen and Bill, or possibly the fire brigade.'

He got another pink fluffy bath towel out of the airing cupboard and wrapped it around her. 'Try kneeling,' he said, and she managed to get on to her knees, and then with Adam holding her to stand upright, swaying, and sit on the side of the bath; and he lifted her gently, round and out, and supported her the two steps to the chair.

They both asked together, 'Are you all right?' and he laughed,

'I've got six months' start on you.' But his injuries had been worse. 'I'm fine,' he said. 'I won't say we should do this more often, but it's nice to know we don't need the fire brigade.'

Her head was reeling. It had been a strain, she had been scared. 'I think you'd better lie down,' he said, and she nodded mutely and let him take her weight. He had said he was fine and she couldn't have walked even along the corridor, but if she didn't lie down she might quite easily flake out. When they reached her room she collapsed on to the bed, and lay on top of the coverlet wrapped in the towel.

The central heating was on, but he turned on the electric fire and she realised that she was shivering. She could have fainted in that bath. If she had floundered around much longer, and not been able to get the water out, this dizziness would have hit her and she could have become unconscious. She said, 'I could have blacked out, I could have drowned.'

'Not you, you're a survivor.' He could be showing more sympathy, she was almost fainting now, she was on the edge of letting go and drifting off. But that jerked her back and she realised that it was true. She wouldn't have slipped down into the water to choke to death, because she wanted so desperately to live that she would have fought like a tiger. She wanted a life with Adam. He had heard her call for help, but if he hadn't and nobody had she would still have crawled out somehow.

Sure I'm a survivor, she thought, but am I a winner? If you don't come for me maybe I'll crawl after you, but where will we go from there?

'You didn't soak that arm you've got in plaster, did you?' he asked.

'Well, of course not, it just got splashed when I slipped.' His shirt was sticking to him, his hair was flat and dark, and she said in some surprise, 'You're soaked!'

'Damp, certainly.' He took off his tie, and then his shirt. Stripped to the waist he was lean and muscular, scarred but strong, and Annie gulped and said, 'You look better than me.'

'You mean temporarily? In normal conditions I can think of no way I would look better than you.'

That made her smile. 'I'm going by the scars.'

'As I keep telling you mine are six months older.'

She looked at her feet, sticking out of the cocoon of the towel, and said ruefully, 'My feet are the best part of me. Hands only look all right, but feet actually work.' She wriggled her toes. 'The rest of me is good in parts.'

'Like the curate's egg,' said Adam.

'The what?'

'An old *Punch* joke.'

'Before my time?'

'About a hundred years.'

'You've worn well,' and he replied with mock gravity. 'Yes, but it's beginning to show.'

'Nothing to do with me, I hope?'

'The thought had occurred.' She laughed, but she wanted to stop talking nonsense and have him sit here beside her, and hold her and talk to her seriously. He looked his age. He had the authority of a man who was mature in every way. She had been plagued by men who were insecure and jealous. With Adam she knew that she could reach the heights, but did he want her up there on the heights with him? Apart from her parents nobody thought that Annie Bennett had much to offer Adam Corbett.

'Where have they gone?' she asked. 'They were supposed to be watching *Casablanca*. They watch it every time it comes on telly because they went to see it when it was a movie and my father thought Mother looked like Ingrid Bergman.'

'Yes.' Adam sounded as though he could still perceive a resemblance. 'Well, she looked at the wrong page in the *Radio Times* and got the wrong day, so they went out for supper instead.'

Her hair was falling over her forehead and when she tried to push it back it felt tacky enough to set in spikes. 'I'm covered in bath oil!' she wailed. She unwrapped herself a little. 'I'm sticking to the towel *and* I've turned green.' Her skin had a faint greasy sheen. 'I'll have to go back and stand under the shower. Hell's bells,' her voice rose in shrill frustration, 'why am I so *helpless*?'

'Because you don't get your brakes fixed,' he said. 'And you're not getting into the bath again tonight. Stay where you are, I'll bring some water in here.'

When he came back carrying another towel, and a tray with a bowl of water, soap, sponge and facecloth, she said, 'Thank you, I should think on the dressing table.' She expected him to leave her to it, but he put the tray on the stool and brought it to the bedside.

Annie was sitting up now, the towel still pulled around her. Her right hand was useless, and she shrugged free from the towel so that she was naked to the waist; she had stopped worrying about how she looked. She reached for the soap, dropped it into the water and then dunked the sponge, and tried to squeeze that with her left hand. It dripped on the bedclothes and Adam took it from her. 'Let me,' he said, and she didn't raise even a token protest.

'Thanks,' she said, and sighed and lay back, closing her eyes because that way she could pretend she was still in hospital, and she must not let herself dwell on the fact that Adam's hands were touching her. Not stroking, just washing off the bath oil quickly and competently.

Although it felt as if she was being caressed. The sponge feathered over the bruises, and then the slightly rougher kiss of the facecloth: arm, fingers, neck, breasts, ribs, flat stomach, legs and feet. A towel blotting her, and she half rolled over so that her back could be washed and dried. The whole length of her spine tingled and she had butterflies inside. She had never known before what the expression 'all a-flutter' meant, but she was sure Adam wasn't trembling. She was no turn-on for him, even when she had been at her almost unblemished best.

'That's got rid of most of it,' he said. 'Can you manage now?'

He handed her the towel and she held it against her face. He was no more embarrassed than a doctor would have been, and she was being ridiculous, blushing, feeling shy. 'What do you wear?' he asked.

'A nightdress.' It was too late to get dressed again, she might as well stay in bed now. 'In there,' in a nightdress case like a satin cushion, that had slid off the bed. When Annie was in these nightgowns they were very suitable, voluminous and press-studded down the front, but when Adam took it out of the case it billowed like a tent.

'Shouldn't be difficult getting you into this,' he said.

'It's for the arm,' she explained. 'It's one of my mother's. I usually wear pyjama tops. My mother uses the bottom halves for dusters because she likes my father in matching sets.' She laughed. 'What do you wear? I mean, if you only wear pyjama trousers——'

'I don't think they'd be my size.'

'Oh, I don't worry about sizes. I just buy what's cheapest in the sales.'

'Well,' he said, 'there'd be no doubt who was wearing the trousers.' He held the nightdress for her, and she got off the bed and they eased it over her plastered arm and Annie slipped in her left hand. She fumbled, trying to pop the press-studs, and Adam fastened them for her, then said, 'Now get back into bed and stay there.'

'I have to go to the bathroom.' She could walk, she would be all right, she was steadier now.

He picked up his shirt and tie and said, 'I'll be back. Don't get trying to clean out the bath, I don't want you pitching in head first.'

What she did want to do was swill the stickiness out of her hair, she didn't think she could sleep until she had. She did that as quickly as possible in the handbasin, and was back in bed with the hairdryer plugged in when Adam came into the room, wearing a thin grey polo-necked sweater now. 'All right?' he asked.

She switched off. 'Yes,' she said, and as he picked up towels and tray she started to say, 'Don't bother,' but if her mother found out that she had got herself stuck in the bath there would be an almighty fuss.

With a pile of wet towels and no bath oil left Annie had obviously had a bath. 'Don't tell them what happened,' she begged. 'If they know I tried to take a bath on my own my mother's not going to leave me alone again as long as my arm's in plaster. So can I just say you helped me?'

'Of course.'

She heard him in the bathroom, the taps running, and she switched on the hairdryer again, blowing her hair into a dark tangled halo. If it had not been for the plaster cast and if her ribs weren't aching, sitting up in bed like this, blowing her hair dry, she could almost imagine she was sexy and pretty and that when Adam came back into the bedroom again he would want to make love to her. She could pretend this was how it always happened, how he always came to her, that all and every night they were together.

When he did come back she said, 'I suppose you couldn't dry my hair for me?'

'You,' he told her, 'have had enough room service for one night,' and she felt like a tiresome child, calling down for another glass of water.

'Sorry,' she said, 'and if you don't wash your hair you too will reek of bath oil in the morning.'

The moment she walked into the bedroom Catrin noticed Annie's flyaway hair. 'You never washed your hair with one hand?' she exclaimed.

'It can be done. I had a bath too, Adam helped me with that.' Her mother gasped and Annie knew that she was shocked. 'It's all right,' she said gaily, 'I'm no sex object at the moment.' But naked was naked to Catrin, who blushed and tried to console herself with,

'Well, I suppose he is almost your husband.'

Only in my dreams, thought Annie. Only in the dreams I'm living in now.

Charlie was one of her visitors next week. He came round at midday on Friday and said, 'You're looking better.' Catrin had let him into the lounge where Annie was sitting with a typewriter, tapping slowly with her left hand. Very laboriously she *was* starting work on her novel, and every day her face was improving, and that was what Charlie meant.

'Well, you won the bet,' he said as he sat down.

'What bet?'

'Don't you remember? That night at the Bodlyn. I bet you couldn't get him.'

She remembered. Eunice Fleming and Adam, and knowing that nothing in the world could stop her walking down that room to Adam and Charlie telling her she was out of her mind.

'Nobody understands it,' said Charlie. 'How did you do it?'

Annie shrugged slightly, and Charlie stayed for

another quarter of an hour, talking about the car he had just bought, a second-hand snip, and looking at Annie as if he was trying to spot something in her that he must have missed before.

When he stood up to go he said, 'You must be dynamite when you really set out to get a man,' and Annie began to laugh as soon as Charlie was out of the room. He thought she had seduced Adam, ensnared him. He thought she had to be the most erotic woman Adam Corbett, who had travelled the world over, had ever met.

She wondered how many others had gone for that explanation. None of her old admirers, because she had never been that passionate, there had always been a reticence in Annie, a holding back. But she only had to recall how it felt when Adam was near, let alone when he touched her, to know that with him it could be different. That this was the man who could set her on fire, so that she would go up like a rocket trailing clouds of glory.

But their relationship continued platonic. He was always considerate, amused and cynical, but he was not her lover, nor did he want to be; and Annie went on teasing and joking, and pretending it didn't cut her to the quick when he kept her at arm's length.

She was making a good physical recovery. She exercised round the garden and her father took her and her mother out in the car, and when Adam came home he always came in to her. She raised her face to be kissed now even if they were alone, and although the kisses were still light and casual it was becoming a very pleasant habit. On fine evenings she would walk round the garden with Adam, and the week after Charlie's visit she asked, 'Can we go up to your room?'

'If you'd like to,' he said.

She took the stone steps carefully, her arm in plaster meant that she was permanently slightly off balance, but she got up with Adam just behind her, and this time she sat in the hide armchair and he brought round the swivel office-type chair that was usually at the desk. Then he poured a glass of wine for them both, and Annie leaned back and looked around.

'I like it up here,' she said. 'I really feel I'm on the mend now.'

'Of course you're on the mend.'

'A lot's happened since I was up here.'

The accident, the ring she wore, the papers on the desk representing some of the work he had done on his book. She had often asked him, 'How's the book going?' and he always replied that it was coming along. So was her own novel. It was not her own story, she was scared to touch on that. The girl was tall and blonde and debby, and the man was a tall dark handsome actor; and the more she wrote about him the more she found herself thinking, Adam would see him off in thirty seconds flat. But she dared not turn her hero into Adam and her heroine into herself, or heaven knew what longings she would spill out on to the paper.

She had fallen asleep on that bed the last time she was up here, and Adam had been in London with Eunice and Annie had been lacerated with jealousy.

'What's the matter?' Adam asked.

'Nothing.'

'Then stop scowling.'

'Was I?' She smiled brightly. 'Your apartment, your—home, shall I tell you how I imagine that?'

'If you like.'

She had seen it in her mind that night so clearly that she had almost believed she could read the number on the phone. Now she described it for him: modern furnishings, abstract pictures on the walls, an oval table, dark like black glass. She had *seen* him and Eunice at that table, but she didn't say that. She went on about a painting of blue and green spheres and triangles floating on a background of paler blue. When she stopped he said, 'That is amazing,' and she felt goosepimples rising on her skin.

'You don't mean I'm right?'

'Every detail,' he paused and she gulped, 'couldn't have been further off the mark. I don't know whose apartment that is, but it sure as hell isn't mine. Mine's full of old furniture and old paintings, I'm an antiques man myself.'

'So I'm not psychic.' She grinned at him and it was all a joke, but all the same she had been right in one of her mind images, Eunice had been with him that night. She drank her winc and knew she could never say, 'By the way, how *is* Eunice these days? Still in Acapulco? When are you expecting her back?'

Somebody would tell her some time, but until they did it was possible to shut Eunice Fleming out of her mind, sometimes for whole days. Although a night rarely passed without the insidious thought coming with the darkness, that Adam had shared nights without number with Eunice and never a one with Annie.

'You're taking me back home tonight, of course?' she said.

'I think so. We wouldn't want your mother wondering if I'm taking advantage of you.'

'You mean me only having one arm like?'

'Something like that.'

One day she might drop her guard and beg, and if she really gave herself away she could lose everything. But until she was forced to think about Eunice, and talk about her, she was going to do her best to pretend that Eunice Fleming did not exist.

Next day was Saturday, and that evening Megan came round to show Annie her new blouse, in white matt silk handpainted with a spray of misty blue harebells. Washable and beautiful, the art teacher at

Barry's school was making them, and Megan was wondering if Annie might be interested in ordering one.

'I think I would,' said Annie. She couldn't wait to get back into the kind of clothes she enjoyed wearing, and as soon as the plaster came off her arm she was going to treat herself to a few new bits and pieces.

'She'll have to be shopping for her trousseau,' said her mother archly, and Megan saw Annie bite her lip and noticed how quickly she said, 'Not yet awhile.'

Catrin went on smiling, 'Well, don't make us wait too long, we want to see our grandchildren. Bronwen was only saying to me yesterday wouldn't it be lovely if the children had your looks and Adam's brains,' and Megan gurgled with laughter,

'That sounds like Bronwen, every compliment a backhander. Now I'd say that any kid who got Annie's brains and Adam's looks would be pretty darn lucky,' and Annie said,

'Thank you; and for heaven's sake, Mother, don't start getting broody for grandchildren. I'm engaged, aren't I? I've got a ring on my finger and that's what you wanted, isn't it? So just let's settle for that for a while.'

A sharpness had crept into her voice that silenced her mother. Then Catrin asked, 'Would you like a coffee, Megan?' and Megan said, 'That would be nice.'

As soon as Catrin had left the room Megan turned to Annie. 'That was a bit snappy, wasn't it?'

'Oh, you know my mother,' said Annie lightly. 'She'd have us up the aisle before Christmas if she had her way, and it just isn't on.'

'You're both for a long engagement, are you?' Megan wasn't smiling and Annie could feel her concern.

'Of course,' she said. 'That's what I want.' The blouse was beside her on the sofa, and she picked it up and inspected it again with fresh concentration. 'It's very pretty. Could she paint a rose on one? I'd like one with a rose for my mother, a sort of thank you for nursing me.'

'Well, of course you know your own business best,' said Megan, and she wasn't talking about blouses. 'And I'm sure you know that Eunice Fleming is still keeping in touch and there was another letter from her yesterday.'

CHAPTER NINE

THAT was it. That shattered the dream where there was no Eunice and Annie had no rival she knew. She wondered when the other letters had come and what Eunice had written in them, what Adam had written to her. He must have talked about his life here, about Annie, and Eunice would be telling him all manner of fascinating things. She would be keeping him in touch with the life that was waiting for him when this little interlude in Llanaven was over.

'Miss Grey sees them,' said Megan as though she was apologising. 'She's still abroad, but she writes her name and address on the back and——' she hesitated, 'he never opens them with the rest of the mail.'

They were not office mail, but Eunice was not sending them here, and Annie wondered if Adam had suggested that, it might have worried Annie's parents. Or if Eunice thought Annie might intercept them because she always had suspected that Annie had a crush on Adam.

And I might, thought Annie, I just might and risk the consequences. I don't believe I could have handed over an envelope with 'Eunice Fleming' written on the back.

'Why shouldn't she write to him?' said Annie. 'They were very good friends.'

They were lovers, living together, and Megan knew that because Annie had told her, and Megan thought Annie was recklessly confident, refusing to admit that Eunice had not given up. But Annie was admitting it, to herself. She knew the danger and she knew the odds. She always had, and Megan had no idea that Annie had nothing to play against Eunice. The ring was phoney. It was all a big pretence, except Annie's feelings for Adam and the superhuman effort it was taking now to stop herself asking, 'How many letters? When did they come, what days? Airmails or thick ones you could put photographs in?' And bursting into tears.

She picked up the blouse, and Megan said, 'I'm sure she could do a rose,' and from then on they talked about nothing in particular until Catrin came back with three cups of coffee on a tray, put down the tray and went off again. Megan handed Annie a cup and took one for herself, but they hardly had time to raise the cups to their lips before Catrin was back.

'See what I've got,' she said. She was smiling again, carrying a flat white box. Megan was standing by the coffee table and Catrin sat down on the sofa beside Annie with the box on her knees. When she took off the lid there was a shimmer of pearls, and she lifted a cloud of misty veiling from the layers of tissue paper.

A shock of recognition hit Annie. It was the veil she should have worn for her wedding to David, and the little pearlseed-encrusted cap. She stared at it disbelievingly. 'It went to Oxfam!'

'The dress did,' said Catrin. 'But I couldn't bear to let this go too. I made this for you, didn't I?' She had embroidered the cap. 'I knew you'd wear it one day when you were a bride. It is pretty, isn't it?'

'It's very pretty,' said Megan. 'It could be a family heirloom.'

Annie had never expected to see it again. She had had conscience pangs over the dress, professionally made by one of Germaine Lloyd Williams' stylists and costing Annie's father the earth, and over this little cap which her mother had embroidered exquisitely and joyfully. But when she stopped the wedding she had believed that the whole bridal outfit had gone to charity.

The veil was short, only waist-length, and when Catrin shook it out it was remarkably uncreased. 'Come on,' Catrin coaxed, 'let me see how it looks.'

Annie sat very still. She couldn't even say, 'I don't want it, because that was a bad time in my life.' It had been a bad time for her mother too. Annie had given her parents a lot of heartache when she jilted David. And why shouldn't Catrin have kept her own handiwork? Why shouldn't she expect Annie to wear it? She had made it for Annie and Annie could hardly say, 'Take it away, I'm never going to be a bride.'

The cap fitted, prettily and snugly as it had the last time, and Annie's dark shining hair curled around it, tendrils falling over her flushed cheeks. 'Now the veil,' said Catrin, head on one side, pursing her lips as she tried to remember. 'How did we fix the veil? I'll get some hairpins.'

'It really is beautiful,' said Megan, examining it closely. 'It would have been wicked to have got rid of it. She's very talented, is your mother.'

Very talented at getting her own way, thought Annie ruefully, but in this case it isn't going to work. A chill was spreading through her. Not because the last time she had worn these things she had been confused and unhappy, but because she would not wear them again. She would never, wearing a bridal veil, walk to meet a man, because Adam would never be waiting for her.

Her mother came back with a handful of hairpins, and Catrin and Megan put on the cap and fiddled with the veil, tucking it in, pinning it down. Megan got the giggles when the cap slipped askew, and Annie kept her lips curved in a small fixed smile.

'It should cover your face when you go into church,' Catrin declared, 'and then you throw it back when you come out.'

'Why?' asked Megan.

'That's the tradition,' said Catrin.

'Then how does he know he's getting the right girl?' Megan wondered, and Catrin chuckled and said that in the old days with a thick veil maybe they got rid of some of the plainer girls that way; and Annie wondered if Eunice was still the right girl for Adam and if this last letter had told him when she would be coming home.

They all heard the front door open. 'Is that your father back?' asked Catrin. Annie and Megan could hear the men's voices clearly, and Annie gasped, 'Don't let Adam come in here and see me in this!'

'But you look very nice,' protested Catrin.

'It would be bad luck,' Annie hissed. 'Go and talk to them for a while,' and as her mother went she bent her head, yanking out hairpins with both hands.

'Steady on!' Megan took over. 'You're going to rip it,' and Annie gulped,

'Get this damn thing off me!'

Megan removed it deftly, folded it quickly, slipped it into the box and put the box behind the sofa. Annie was smoothing her hair down with her left hand. She would not for the world have had Adam see her decked as a bride. If he did heaven knew what he might think. Maybe that she was deluding herself that he could be quietly coerced into marriage. There was no man less likely to be coerced into anything, but it would be horribly shaming if he felt it necessary to remind her what their relationship was.

'You are a funny girl,' said Megan. 'I can't see that it would have mattered. Can they come in now?'

The men had been at a British Legion meeting. A guest speaker had had to cancel at the last minute and Douglas Bennett had persuaded Adam to stand in. Douglas was in good spirits. Adam had been a great success with the members, most of whom had known his father, all of whom had heard of him, the local boy who'd made good. They had had a splendid evening, Douglas declared, Adam's talk had been something they would all remember.

He went on telling Catrin and the girls this as Adam came and kissed Annie's cheek. She smiled back at him, pale and composed, and from Megan's expression she felt she could read Megan's thoughts.

Megan was thinking that Adam could be a cold lover, because there was too much self-control there. 'I can't see any woman breaking through that reserve, and I believe Annie knows it,' Annie read in Megan's eyes. She could see pity too, and although she went on smiling the smile must have been wistful, because Adam sat down beside her, and took her hand and said, 'You're looking tired.'

Concern and kindness were always there, but she didn't want him to hold her hand as he might a child's. She wanted him to lace his fingers with hers, tightening until it hurt; press her palm with his thumb as though the feel of her flesh was a sensuous delight to him. He was that to her. It was all she could do to make her hand lie still in his, and when Megan said, 'I suppose I'd better be getting along,' Annie stood up too. 'I'll see you to the door.'

'Ask about a blouse with a rose on,' she said, and Megan said sure she would and she was sure it could be done. ''Bye for now,' she said, and Annie stood watching the car draw away from the kerb, until she remembered the veil and thought her mother might start looking for the box, and making arch little comments. Then she hurried back into the lounge, but everyone was sitting where she had left them.

Her father was still talking about tonight. 'They tried to book him in again,' said Douglas Bennett, 'but he wasn't committing himself on that.' He watched Adam, then looked at Annie. 'We shall be losing you, shan't we, before long?'

He didn't mean they would be losing Annie, he meant that Adam would only be editor of the *Bugle* for a few months. That had always been obvious, and now Adam said, 'Off the record, Glyn Rees will take over at the beginning of December.'

Her mother and father thought she knew, but Adam hadn't told her the date, and this made the prospect of winter bleaker. If they kept up their pretence he would probably write and phone and he might come visiting, but their lives would be separate. He wouldn't be almost under the same roof. When he was gone Annie wouldn't be able to tell herself that maybe tonight, or tomorrow, he would look at her and want her.

'Why don't you get married before Adam goes?' asked Catrin, and went on in the silence that followed her words, 'Well, why not? We had to wait because my father was ill and all on his own and I couldn't leave him, when I was young family responsibilities came first, but that doesn't mean I don't regret the years that we wasted. You could get married very soon if you wanted to. That would be wonderful, to be married and young. Why don't you show Adam——' She looked round for the box and the veil, and Annie panicked because Adam would think she had been talking about this, with her friend and her mother, dressing up as a bride, plotting to have Catrin angling for a date. Of course he would get out of it, but he must not think that was what had happened.

She said, 'No, I've told you *no*. Don't rush us. Leave us alone.' She had to stop her mother arguing, even appealing to Adam. She said desperately, 'That was what happened last time. Don't rush us this time.'

'I'm sorry.' Catrin made a helpless little gesture, but the warning struck home. She began to gather up the coffee cups and Douglas helped her, picking up the tray, going with her to the kitchen.

'*I'm* sorry,' Annie said to Adam. 'Just shrug it off if she starts up again. Tell her that with my track-record you consider a long engagement absolutely necessary.'

'There's a point.'

She had to keep things as they were as long as she could. If her mother started planning a wedding Adam might decide he couldn't go on with the phoney engagement and that anyhow Annie was almost strong enough now to stand on her own feet. She looked at her ring and said, 'But I would be grateful if we could carry on with this.'

'Why not?' He sounded as though they were discussing some small service that was hardly worth mentioning. 'As long as you like. Give me a little warning when you're ready to jilt me and I'll adopt your parents.'

Eunice obviously didn't mind, she knew it didn't mean anything, and Adam thought that before long Annie would find another man who wanted to marry her and whom she wanted to marry. She couldn't say, 'There'll never be anyone but you,' because he wouldn't believe her, he wouldn't want to believe her. Instead she said wryly, 'You may have to adopt them. They've adopted you.'

'I'd like that, a family in my old home town.'

With Annie as his sister? She said, 'You've got it.' But no sister, and don't bring Eunice home or I'll personally poison her tea.

The joke was bitter, twisting her lips, and he said again, 'You're looking tired. I think you should go to bed.'

It was late enough and his concern was comforting, but the real comfort she wanted was his arms around her and the touch of his lips. She said, 'Right you are, but then you always are.' She tried to sound flippant, lifting herself off the sofa, but when Adam stood to help her she said, 'It's been a long day.'

'That bad?'

He had kept Eunice's letters to read later, putting them aside from the office mail, opening them when he was alone, and if she said, 'I hear you heard from Eunice yesterday,' he would know that the office was gossiping and Miss Grey could colour up beetroot if he questioned her. 'Just boredom setting in,' she said.

'Poor pet!' He treated her like a pet, but when he held her, as always, his closeness blew her mind so that she was hardly conscious of anything but the need to cleave to him as though she was only whole when they were together. If he had kissed her she would have kissed back with all her heart and soul, but he only smiled at her, and she made a mournful funny face.

'I am down,' she said. 'I'm feeling low, I need cheering up. Couldn't you just brush my hair or rub my back or something?'

'I don't think you're up to that kind of cheering up yet,' he said. 'If things get out of hand it could set you back weeks.'

They were fooling, this was talk that meant nothing. 'Promise?' she said, and he burst out laughing, and she said, 'Just you wait till I've got two good arms.'

Catrin came into the room while they were still laughing, and Adam said, 'I'll see you tomorrow, now get some rest.'

'You too,' said Annie. Dream of me, damn you, she thought. I shall dream of you, and toss and turn aching for you, so why should you sleep easy?

Catrin sighed as Adam closed the door behind him and said, 'I don't know why you're comparing Adam with David, David was never half the man Adam is, and this is nothing like the last time; and I think you're being very silly, talking about not being rushed, and letting Adam leave here without fixing a date for the wedding. A man like Adam, there could be other girls.' Only the one, thought Annie, but she's more than enough. 'I'm not saying he'll forget you,' said her mother, 'but——'

'I'll just have to make sure that he doesn't,' said Annie with a forced and feigned confidence.

She knew she was pathetic. What could she do to make Adam remember her the way she wanted to be remembered, so that he missed her all the time? And now that she knew when he was going the days seemed to move faster. Each one ticked off on the calendar meant that time was running out. When her arm was out of plaster she would go back to her job, and for a little while she would be part of the 'new' *Bugle*. She was looking forward to that, but it was all bringing the day he would be leaving here closer.

Under Adam's editorship the *Bugle* was earning a reputation for some first-class journalism. Every edition sold out quickly and readers' letters came thick and fast. People were taking notice of it, and during the next few weeks when Annie dropped into the office to say hello and usually to have lunch with Megan she could feel the buzz in the air. Even old stick-in-the muds like John Hogan, still puffing on his foul pipe, seemed to have livened up.

Something else Annie could sense, and that was that Miss Grey and Megan were not the only ones who knew that letters from Eunice Fleming were arriving for Adam. Nobody mentioned them, and Adam never had, but she felt that most of her colleagues believed that when Adam left here Annie could kiss him goodbye.

'We'll be sorry to see Adam go, he'll be missed,' she was told more than once. No announcement had been made, but everybody seemed to know that he would be leaving before long, and without his driving force the *Bugle* would soon revert to just another provincial weekly. For years to come the staff would hark back to the six months when Adam Corbett was editor, when they were all, somehow, producing such cracking good work. And it didn't help Annie to know that she would be reminiscing with them and missing Adam like nobody else did.

'When he does go will you go with him?' Megan asked her bluntly as they ate omelettes in a café near the *Bugle* where they often lunched.

'No', said Annie. 'Well, not for a while.' She was

hoping to start work again next week and there wasn't a chance of her leaving with Adam. Nothing had changed in the seven weeks since she came out of hospital, except that she had made a good physical recovery.

But so had Adam. In the last few days he had been driving a car, a Porsche with automatic control, so that he no longer needed taxis or 'lifts'. He had brought Annie into town this morning and last week they had driven out to a lonely beach she had always loved, off the tourist trail, and they had walked and talked with the salt air on their faces. Sometimes it seemed to Annie that they must have discussed everything under the sun, except Eunice. She usually did most of the talking—she was a natural chatterer—but Adam always listened as though what she was saying interested him, and he talked too. She told him all manner of things, but never that she loved him and that when he went away all the joy of living would go with him.

It was Friday. On Monday the plaster was coming off her arm, and she was crazy to imagine that would make any lasting difference. Except set her free to start work again, to move around unfettered. Adam would still look on her as an amusing and likeable girl, a bit scatty but a promising writer. He was encouraging about her novel, she showed him bits of it sometimes during their evenings together in the studio. But having the cast off her arm was not going to make her suddenly so sexy that he couldn't keep his hands off her. When he left here people might even go on believing for a while that she was going to marry him, but if he ever kissed her properly, just once, she would probably die of surprise and delight.

Megan would have been surprised if Annie had said, 'Sure I'll be going with him.' Annie had given her the answer she expected and she said, 'Why don't you both come round tomorrow night, I'll cook something special?' That was nice, Annie thought, Megan was sorry for her and wanting to do something, if it was only cook a special meal.

'Adam's away tomorrow,' said Annie. 'He'll be back Sunday evening, but I don't know what time.'

'Oh!' For a moment Megan was very still, then she became briskly animated. 'Next weekend, then, or any night, just say when,' and they were halfway through their sweet course when she enquired, very casually, 'Did you know Eunice Fleming was in London? There was a letter with a London postmark on Wednesday.'

Adam had told Annie and her parents earlier in the week that he had business contacts to meet, but now she knew that he would be seeing Eunice and the cheesecake tasted like ashes. 'Didn't Miss Grey steam it open?' Annie smiled, and Megan almost blushed.

It seemed that her mother had taken to heart what Annie had said about not being rushed this time, because she hadn't mentioned fixing a wedding date again, but Annie suspected she had talked about it with her father; because it was her father who asked, 'Any idea when the wedding's going to be?' as Annie was trying to read the Sunday papers on Sunday morning.

She had hardly slept the previous two nights. Thoughts of Adam with Eunice had kept her on the rack, and now sadness had settled on her like the exhaustion of a fatal illness. 'No idea at all,' she said.

'You do love him?' Douglas found it harder to talk about love than Catrin, and his voice was gruff.

'Oh yes,' said Annie.

'And he loves you. That was the first thing I asked him. "Do you love her?" I said.'

Annie had to smile. 'You mean before you went into the matter of his bank balance?'

'Of course.' And of course Adam had said yes, he could hardly have said no. 'Nobody's expecting you to get married next week,' her father went on, 'but your mother and I feel it wouldn't be a bad idea if you settled on a date before Adam leaves.'

If she got into this discussion she would weep. Her father was looking at her with such concern, asking her, 'Did you sleep well last night? You're looking rather pale this morning—you're not worried about anything, are you?' and she could never tell him, 'I didn't sleep very well because Adam was sleeping with another woman.'

She said, 'Of course I'm not worrying. But I still can't rest really comfortably with this thing on my arm. When it comes off tomorrow I'll be fine, then I'll be really cured. Don't nag me today, eh? It's been a long two months.'

He smiled at her and shook his head and left it at that.

It was late Sunday evening when Adam came back. Her mother and father were drinking their milky nightcaps and Annie had been listening for a long time for the sound of his car. She wasn't even sure that he would be back tonight. He had said he probably would, but Eunice might have helped him change his mind and he might have gone straight into the office in the morning. He had to be back by tomorrow night because he was appearing on regional TV.

'That's Adam,' she said, and a few minutes later he came through the back door from the garden and into the little sitting room. Catrin got up to welcome him with a motherly hug and Annie wondered if Eunice's perfume would cling to his jacket.

If it did she thought she would be sick, but it didn't. He took her hand and he kissed her cheek, and his lips were cool. Annie smiled up at him and he looked down at her with just the right moment of eye contact that could have been an unspoken message. It wasn't, of course, it was all part of the pretence.

'Have a good weekend?' she asked. 'Meet anyone special, do anything exciting?'

He had commissions lined up. He talked about them briefly and her father and mother were impressed, and so was Annie. He would be right into the thick of things again within days of leaving here, within weeks he would be as big a name as ever. Of course, it was impressive, and of course he never mentioned Eunice.

Then her father asked jovially, 'When *are* you two getting married?' and Annie sagged back in her seat.

'Ask Annie,' said Adam.

That was not fair. She knew what she had to say, but it would have been easier for him to say it. 'We've all the time in the world,' she said.

'Next summer?' her father persisted.

'I was nearly a June bride last time,' said Annie tartly. 'I'm not sure summer is my season.'

'It's a long time to wait,' said Catrin. 'A lot could happen before then.' She meant that Adam would be on the other side of the world with other things on his mind, and Annie muttered,

'Ain't that the truth?'

'Make it midsummer,' said Adam. By next summer he would have expected Annie to have found someone else to take his place as her minder, or have made a firm stand for independence. By then he would be gone anyway.

'Maybe,' said Annie. 'And now let's shut up about wedding dates. I think tomorrow will be an interesting day. My cast comes off and Adam's on the telly, and I need a good night's sleep to get ready for all that excitement.'

She kissed them all good night. She kissed Adam as he had kissed her, her lips brushing his cheek. Then she went up to her bedroom and she heard him leave the house not long after. The light was on in the loft, a pale searchlight piercing the sky, and tonight she slept better than she had the previous two nights, because at least she knew where he was and that he was alone . . .

Annie watched Adam on television with her mother and father, just the three of them. It was a late-night talk show, three men and one woman, answering questions from the audience and Adam was far and away the best of the bunch. He got the applause every time. His anecdotes were the funniest, his comments were bang on target. He was as good as Annie had expected him to be, and she almost wished he wasn't, because it proved what they all believed, that he was out of her league.

All the *Bugle* staff would be watching, and everybody who had met him since he came back to Llanaven. Bronwen was taping it on video, and after Adam had gone Annie might persuade her father to buy or rent a video, and then she could see Adam again whenever she liked. And that might make her suicidal if she knew he wasn't coming back.

Megan phoned when the programme ended. 'Wasn't he great? Barry and I thought he was terrific.' And Annie was hardly back in the sitting room before the phone was ringing again.

'Have you been watching our man on TV?' It was a woman's drawling voice.

'Who is it?' Annie knew who it was.

'Eunice Fleming.' Eunice couldn't have received the transmission in London, so she had to be down here, maybe in the studio. Annie bit her lip hard and said, 'Good, wasn't he?'

'Of course he was,' said Eunice. 'I haven't seen the programme yet, but a friend's taping it for me.'

'It is live. Adam isn't here.'

'I know that, it's you I want to speak to about this engagement nonsense.' Eunice knew what was behind it. They must have discussed it over the weekend, and she sounded as though she had no patience with such a daft arrangement. 'I suppose Adam needed some amusement during his sabbatical.' She was sneering now, Annie could imagine the curl of her lip; and the way she was looking down her nose as she had in the Ladies' in the Bodlyn Arms when she was ordering Annie to stop pestering Adam. 'But it's high time the farce ended,' she snapped.

It was a farce and some time it would end, but not because Eunice was throwing her weight about. 'Tell Adam,' said Annie.

'You tell him I'll be down tomorrow,' snapped Eunice, and Annie put down the receiver.

She would not be bullied. Adam would not let this become gossip that would hurt her parents and make a fool of Annie. He was too fond of them all. She had to tell herself that to stop herself panicking.

'Who was it?' her mother asked as she carried the two empty mugs into the kitchen.

'Somebody else from the office,' said Annie, and she hovered in the hall in case Eunice should call back before her mother and father went up to bed. She was still standing by the hall table when they said good night to her.

'Don't stay up too late,' her father said, and her mother smiled because Annie was all dressed up and waiting for Adam.

She had intended waiting for him to come home and saying, 'Look, two arms!' She had wanted to tell him she thought he had been great on TV. She was nearly as good as new now, her arm was straight although the skin was wrinkled. She had soaked rich skin cream into it and she was wearing the red dress with the white fringed collar, and now she was going upstairs to slosh on some more of her favourite perfume.

She would have tried to make some sort of celebration of tonight. He might have made love to her. She might have succeeded in blotting Eunice from his mind for a while, if only Eunice hadn't phoned.

Tomorrow Eunice would be here, telling Annie's parents at least that Adam had no intention of marrying Annie and that Annie had always known that. Now they would have to talk about Eunice and it would be the first time Annie had said her name, and when she did she felt that she might as well hand back her crystal ring.

She didn't know what time Adam would return. She hadn't seen him since last night and she had probably made too much of today in her own mind. Having the cast taken off her arm had seemed important because now she was pretty again; and Adam liked her, they were close and caring friends.

She wouldn't mind if the sex was as lighthearted as their relationship had always been. She didn't expect it to mean anything lasting to him, but tonight she had been fairly sure that he wouldn't turn her out of the loft, he would let her stay. Why shouldn't he take what she was offering? She was a more than willing adult, and he would never guess that she wanted him so desperately that she could make the memory of a night last a lifetime.

She dabbed on more perfume, then picked up her purse with comb and lipgloss, and went out of the house. She would wait in the loft, and she would say nothing about Eunice for a while. She would pretend for a while that Eunice had not phoned and was not coming tomorrow. For pity's sake, Eunice had had months, years, of Adam as her lover, and the future as well, and she was not robbing Annie of her one night.

There had surely never been such a night for stars. There couldn't be a single cloud up there, the whole world seemed still and waiting. The garden was in darkness, but the sky was a brilliant glittering dome. Annie caught her breath when she stepped out of the house, and almost tripped crossing the lawn, because she was staring up at the sky.

It seemed a pity to put on the light in the loft. Through the skylight the stars were still breathtaking, and she would have preferred not too much illumination for her seduction scene. She was trying to seduce him, and he was going to find that amusing and it would be harder if she saw him smile. But he would turn on the light anyway, as soon as he came in, so she did.

She was as nervous as a drama student before an audition that could make or break. She couldn't keep still. She wandered round the room, straightening papers on the desk, looking at closed drawers and wondering if Eunice's letters were there. If she had found a letter she would have dropped it like a stinging thing, she couldn't bear to read what Eunice wrote to Adam, but she could imagine the letters being here in this room. She thought she could smell another perfume, not her own, and that was pure fancy like 'seeing' Adam's apartment and getting it completely wrong.

She sat down, and two minutes later jumped up again and went on pacing the room, going round and round in circles, until she made herself stand still. She must keep calm, and stop jittering. If she could keep her head and say the right things, and flirt and fool, the one thing would surely lead to another and they would spent the night together.

What she must not do was burst into tears and tell him she hadn't known what wanting was until she met him, and that although he would go away and forget making love with her she would remember, every night, every kiss and every caress.

She alternated between hope—she *was* sexy, men fancied her so much that she had never had to make the running before; even the ones who hadn't really liked her, like Huw, had fancied her. And fear. Because Adam might feel that he had committed himself enough with Annie and that even the most casual sexual encounter could cause complications.

He might not want her. He had had a long day and he might just want to get some sleep. He might be exasperated at finding her here and pack her off, no matter how frantically she tried to be seductive.

She had a small mirror in her purse, and she took it out and curled tendrils of her hair round her finger, then she put some more gloss on her lips, and looked at her reflection, trying to brainwash some confidence into herself. She was pretty, she was sexy, but no more than a million others and not in the running at all compared with Eunice.

She was sitting cross-legged on the divan bed, and up there were a myriad stars. It was like the crystal cave, and she wished she could believe in magic. She wished she had brought some of her father's whisky over here to give herself a little courage, but the last time she had said, 'Please make love to me,' had been the night of the barbecue, and she didn't want Adam recalling that.

She tried to rehearse what she was going to say. She closed her eyes and imagined him coming into the room and how it would go from there, but the only thing that stayed clear was the moment when he touched her. The words, the preliminaries, got jumbled, but from there it was sure and right and wonderful. She lay waiting, dreaming her dreams, until she heard the car, then her eyes opened wide and she jerked upright.

By the time footsteps sounded on the stone steps she was smiling. Please let him look pleased to see me. Please don't let him say, 'Have you any idea what time it is?'

He smiled, and that was one prayer answered. Annie sat up straighter as he dropped a briefcase on the desk. 'Do I look different?' she asked. 'See—two arms!' She lifted them both, although her right arm was still stiff.

'It's a good number,' he said.

'Eunice phoned.' She had not meant to tell him till morning, although it would have troubled her until she had. She hoped this didn't mean that she was getting so used to running to Adam with her troubles that she did it instinctively, because that would have to stop, and soon. Her voice was light when she mimicked Eunice. 'She said she understood that you needed something to entertain you while you were stuck out here in the backwoods, but that it's time we called the farce off. Oh, and she's arriving tomorrow.' But when she asked him, 'Will she tell everybody that it was just a pretence?' her anxiety showed.

'No,' he said. He sounded confident about that, but Eunice had sounded resentful enough to let slip a few hints even if she had been sworn to secrecy, and Annie grimaced, 'You're sure.'

'Very sure. She doesn't know.'

That meant he hadn't discussed it with Eunice. Eunice believed he *was* engaged to Annie. No wonder she had been spitting mad, even if she had thought it was unlikely to last. The little pocket mirror was under Annie's fingers, and her ring scratched against it as she twisted her hand.

She was gasping before, but now she stared down at the graze on the glass, her mouth falling open, because crystals didn't cut glass. Only diamonds cut.

'It's diamonds!' she gulped, and waited for Adam to exclaim. But he didn't—he knew. He had bought her diamonds. She had been wearing something fabulous. 'Now I'll have to give it back.' Of course she would. 'Shall you give it to Eunice?'

'No,' he said again, and she looked down at the ring, hardly daring to speak.

'She's been around all the time, hasn't she? What with letters and that. Are you very fond of her?'

Adam spoke slowly, quietly. 'When I thought I was dying I thought of the reasons I wanted to live. Your priorities sort themselves out under those circumstances, but I never thought of Eunice at all.'

She almost told him, 'I thought of you, I only thought of you,' but then he said, 'This midsummer marriage, shall we go through with it?' and she was gasping again. 'It could work out very well.'

He was looking at her with that direct gaze that made her feel he could read every thought in her head, but she couldn't read him. 'We could get accustomed to each other in a very satisfactory fashion,' he said.

'Could we?' She wanted to get accustomed to everything about him because she was crazy for him, but why did he want to marry her? Did he want a wife to hold off the Eunices? She said, 'This is very flattering and very surprising. You mean, marriage for real?' The crystal ring was diamonds, no pretending any more. 'But *why*? I suppose I'm pretty enough, and I still think you're the most attractive man I've ever met. We could have had an affair, I'd understand that, but are you sure you want to marry me? You'd never be sure you could trust me. I mean, you think I conned you about losing my memory.'

'I believe what you told me,' he said. 'I'd trust you with my life.'

'You would?'

'Of course. I love you more than my life.'

Annie reached out a hand and he took it and sat down beside her, and she gasped, '*You* love *me*?'

'Don't ever doubt it.'

She wasn't doubting, now she believed in magic, but she had to ask, 'Since when?'

'If I'd known you before I went over that landmine you would have kept me alive.' She was drinking in his words, leaning close to listen, her eyes fixed on his face. 'When I first met you I thought you were an attractive girl, so life was easy for you. Then, very soon, I knew that I liked you, I wanted to take care of you, but I didn't realise how totally I'd fallen in love with you until I came back that weekend, after finishing with Eunice, and they told me you'd crashed your car.

'For a moment I thought they were telling me you were dead, and it was like the world ending.' His fingers tightened around hers as if he would never let her go, then he smiled. 'You, lying in that hospital bed, were the most beautiful sight I'd ever seen.'

'Beautiful?' she had to echo.

'Because you were alive and breathing.'

'But I looked so dreadful!'

'Not to me. If you'd stayed disfigured, crippled, it would have made no difference to the way I felt about you.'

She had known how she felt about him, although she had hidden the depth of her caring under a façade of flippancy, but she had never dreamed that he could love her so much. 'You never told me,' she said, 'I told you.'

'You told me you fancied me, which is a bloody silly word and a million light years from how I feel about you. I thought we'd better get round to my way of thinking gradually. You're wearing my ring.' There would be another ring now, a wedding ring, and she would wear both with such pride. 'And you were in no state to form any other attachments, so time was on my side.

'But don't imagine it's been easy keeping my hands off you for the past two months, and from now on I'm going to prove to you that you'd enjoy being my wife.'

He kissed her, deep and tender, and she went limp with delight at his taste and touch. Every bit of her hungered for him. Being loved by Adam would be like feasting after starving. 'And there's another reason why you should marry me,' he told her.

'You mean my parents?' She didn't want the kissing to stop. She lay, looking up at him, her lips a breath away from his lips.

'I mean,' he said, 'that I'd kill any man who took you from me.'

Annie looked into his eyes and saw such a blaze of love that she knew she did matter more to him than his life, and she smiled, 'Are you planning to seduce me?'

'Yes.'

'There's a funny thing—I thought I might try to seduce you. Just for tonight, I thought, just for starters.'

'Not just for tonight,' he said. 'For good. For ever.'

He kissed her again, gently at first, and she shivered in anticipation, loving the exploration of his hands. She wanted to make it last, just lying here and letting these incredible sensations happen to her. But her arms went around him, and her body took over her mind, suffusing her with a savage sensuousness. She knew then that she had never made love before. No man had ever taken her to these heights and she had never given with such passion. Adam knew how to make her so happy that she wept and laughed together, and sometimes she was seducing him so that he moaned, 'Oh God, you're so beautiful,' and she whispered, 'So are you,' and she clung to him through a shared and exquisite ecstasy that seemed as though they would hold the embrace for ever.

Afterwards she lay, drowsy and still in his arms. As she turned her head he smiled at her and she began 'This midsummer marriage——'

'Yes?' He put his lips to the soft swell of her breast and she felt her toes curl and her stomach going hollow with desire. Every time I look at him, she thought, I want him. Thank heavens he felt the same, because the way he was looking at her now she had better say what she was going to say quickly.

'Do you think we could make it sooner?' she said, and Adam smiled again.

'I think we'd better, I'll get a licence tomorrow,' and she hardly had time to tell him,

'I love you with all my heart,' before again, and marvellously, there was no need for words at all.